JACK AT THE LODGE
A Jack of All Trades novel

DH Smith

Earlham Books

Published 2020 by Earlham Books
Book design & cover art by Lia at Free Your Words
(*www.FreeYourWords.com*)

ISBN: 978-1-909804-44-9

Chapter 1

Jack pushed the wheelbarrow through the side door, making his way between the house and the side fence, heading for the back garden. The wheelbarrow contained just the items to mark out the site. A couple of days' work here, if the weather held. Today was fine, one of those half sunny spring days, a little chilly, early April, still not sure of itself.

When he'd been here the other day to price the work, he had measured the width of the passage between house and fence. It was wide enough, just about, to get the cement mixer through. Which was a relief, otherwise he'd be mixing by hand. Hard work, and he'd had a couple of dizzy spells recently. One of them when he'd been mixing concrete.

Probably nothing much, but he should do less grunt stuff until the bug went. So it was good the cement mixer could get in. He had digging to do, but he would take it easy. Have breaks. Ration the work.

Jack came out into the garden, by the patio which had tubs of daffodils and primroses. There was a brick barbecue at one end and in the centre a slatted wooden table with six matching chairs, lined on either side. The house was a bed and breakfast and on warmer days they ate outside, hardly today, though a column ash tray with a few fag ends showed smokers braved the elements.

Beyond the patio was the lawn. On either side, in the beds along the fences, were dying daffodils and tulips just breaking bud. Amidst them, wallflowers had a sprinkling of

1

flowers; a warm day would have them opening. The garden was long, the railway in the cutting behind the back fence.

The bottom half was a vegetable patch with a woman working in it. She was 40-ish, hair blonde and curly, black and grey creeping into the roots. The woman was wearing jeans and a yellow t-shirt, her complexion a mild brown, suggesting mixed race parentage. The ground was freshly dug and raked to a fine tilth. She had laid a string line across it, and was scoring a shallow depression by the string with a hoe. Beside her was a straw basket containing seed packets and a trowel.

The French windows were open. Jack would need to bring the electric cable through them for the cement mixer, hopefully tomorrow. It wasn't that big an area to concrete, just the base for a garden shed. Not that arduous, except those dizzy spells recently. Jack had gone to the doctor, who'd sent him for a blood test. Yesterday, he'd had a phone call from the surgery for an appointment later this morning.

He considered cancelling the appointment, but the surgery wasn't far. Inertia kept the appointment. Stupid going in over nothing, just some bug. It would go in a few days. The digging was the only hard work to be done. Pace it.

Jack left the wheelbarrow and went to the edge of the lawn.

'Good morning, Cleo,' he called to the woman in the vegetable bed. 'I'm all set.'

She stopped scoring the soil, and rested on the hoe.

'It's only half seven,' she said, glancing at her wristwatch. 'I wasn't expecting you for another half an hour.'

'I've a doctor's appointment at eleven,' he said. 'So I thought I'd get going early.'

'Nothing serious, I hope?'

'I won't die on you,' he said with a shrug.

'I hope not.' She looked around her and at her watch again. 'I've just time to put in these beetroot seeds, then I'll have to get on with breakfast. I've a full house today. Would you like coffee and toast?'

'That'd be great.'

Jack had brought a thermos as he never knew what was on offer. Best not to assume. He'd met Cleo two days ago. He quoted a price, and was barely prepared for her haggling. She questioned everything, pushing him lower and lower. He was about to pull out as he was at his limit, when she accepted. Tight wasn't the word for this job. He'd be in pocket if the weather held, but a day or two of rain and he'd be working for less than minimum wage.

Cleo was pleasant once the deal was agreed but he wouldn't want to cross her. He'd heard her on the phone berating a butcher. So it wasn't just him.

'I'll get started,' he said.

Jack pushed the wheelbarrow to one corner, where lawn and vegetable patch met the flower bed along the fence. Four bricks had been placed out on the grass, each at the corner of the rectangle to be concreted. The concrete would need to dry for a week, then the shed would be erected.

The brick corners were approximate; he would have to mark out an accurate perimeter, two inches wider all round than the shed. Or five centimetres. Jack switched easily from centimetres to inches. Materials were metric these days but it was good to handle both, as some of his older customers hadn't caught up.

There were four wooden pegs in the wheelbarrow, to replace the bricks. And a ball of string to go round them, marking out the site accurately. Each corner had to be a right-angle. Make an error there and the shed could overlap the concrete base in one corner. He had a large wooden right-angled triangle intended for jobs like this, he was sure,

3

but couldn't find it, buried in that mythical somewhere in his lock-up.

Fortunately, there were other ways.

A woman came out of the French windows rubbing her eyes at the sunlight. She sank into one of the patio chairs and took out a packet of cigarettes. She was mid 30s, a little overweight, brown hair down to her shoulders, wearing a navy skirt and a white blouse.

'Who's in room 2, Cleo?'

Cleo was hoeing soil over the seeds she'd just sown. She looked across.

'A chap called Clyde. Why?'

The woman lit her cigarette. 'He snores like a tank.' She sucked in deeply and then exhaled. 'I didn't get a wink of sleep. When's he leaving?'

'He's staying another two nights, Beryl.'

'I can't take another night of him. You've got to move him.'

Cleo leaned on the hoe and bit her lip. 'OK,' she said, after a pause. 'He can have my room.'

'Where will you sleep?'

Cleo shrugged. 'I'll take his.'

'You'll be next to him.'

'Don't worry, Beryl. If it's too much,' said Cleo, 'I'll sleep on the couch in the lounge.'

Jack couldn't help overhearing. Full house it seemed. He knew there were five upstairs rooms: Cleo's and four guest rooms.

Cleo crossed the lawn with the hoe and basket and sat down at the patio table.

'Sorry about Clyde,' she said. 'I didn't know he made such a racket.'

'I thought about coming downstairs and sleeping on the couch myself,' said the woman. 'Should've done. He had this repeat pattern. He'd take a deep snore, like a dragon down a coal mine. Then a break, maybe two seconds. Each time, I'd think that's it, he's done. But no, there'd come a double rumble and off he'd go again. I went into his room a couple of times, gave him a shake. Nothing would wake him, stank like a brewery, but the shove stopped him for five minutes. Then he'd be off again. What a night!'

'What can I say?' said Cleo. 'I'll move him tonight.'

The woman didn't reply, so perhaps she was mollified. Not easy running a bed and breakfast, thought Jack. Like his own job. The work was straightforward. Pity about the customers.

'I'll get the breakfast ready,' said Cleo. 'Quarter of an hour, Beryl.' She went in the French windows.

Jack had hammered in two wooden pegs parallel with the vegetable garden, and had tied a line of string between them. That was the length of the shed plus a few inches. Now he needed a right angle for one of the sides. He measured four feet along the string with his tape measure. Jack pushed in a 6 inch nail. He was measuring three feet down from the peg when he was aware of the woman standing over him.

'Pythagoras' theorem?' she said.

'So they say. But I never met the man. Just learnt it from an old brick layer,' he said. 'Just do 3, 4, 5 sides and you'll get a right angle. I told my daughter; she said Pythagoras discovered it. Now what did she say?' He bit his lower lip in concentration. 'The square on the something or other...' he stopped. 'What's the long diagonal called?'

'Hypotenuse.'

'That's it. The square on the hypotenuse is equal to the sum of the squares on the other two sides.' He laughed in mini-triumph. 'Not bad for a Monday morning.'

'Three squared plus four squared equals five squared,' said the woman.

'Smart, those Greeks,' said Jack. 'All I know is that it works.' He put in the second nail. 'So let's see if I've got it

5

right first time. The diagonal between the nails should be five feet.' He stretched out the tape.

Beryl had got down on her knees. 'Five feet one and a half inches,' she read off the tape. 'So this nail has to come in one and a half inches. I'll do it.'

She moved the nail along the tape.

'Great,' said Jack. 'Five feet exactly. One right angle. Thanks for that.'

'You only need one more,' she said. 'And the other two will fit. Let me help. Saves me lighting another fag. I'm trying to give up but I wasn't able to sleep a wink last night. You heard what I said to Cleo?'

'The snorer. Yeh.' It had reminded him of his drinking days. Alison, his ex, had moved him into the spare room because of his snoring. That was before she kicked him out.

'What do you do?' he said, to change the subject.

'I'm an auditor.'

'Ah! That's why you're good at sums.'

He'd measured the four feet from the second peg. She put in the nail.

'What a team!' she declared. 'It must have been like this building the pyramids.'

'A somewhat bigger base needed.'

'Same principle for the Great Pyramid at Giza,' she said. 'Just a lot more string.'

Quickly they got the second right angle.

'The shed is twelve feet wide, plus two inches at either end...' Jack measured to where the third wooden peg should go. He hammered it in lightly in case it had to be moved. Then the fourth. And ran the line round the four pegs.

'That should be four right angles,' he said. 'Let's check the last two.'

'OK, Pharaoh,' said Beryl with a mock salute, taking three nails out of the wheelbarrow.

'I don't think the Pharaohs ever got down on their knees with a tape,' he said.

'If they did, it would be solid gold and quite useless,' she said. 'More likely, they'd turn up in a chariot, and five thousand workers would press their heads to the sand.'

She mock bowed to the ground.

Was she flirting? thought Jack. Did she have a husband somewhere? Such thoughts, so early. Work.

They checked the 3, 4, 5s on one of the new corners, with Beryl putting in a nail at each measurement.

'Spot on,' he said as he measured the 5. 'Three right angles. The last one has to be one.'

'Let's check anyway,' she said, 'to see if we've found the exception.'

He measured, she put in the nails at the 3 feet and 4 feet lengths along the string at either side of the angle. Jack measured the diagonal. 'And another 5! Four right angles. Bingo!'

'It's so beautifully primitive,' she said. 'Geometry. Or is it trigonometry? One of them, or both. Much better than staring into a screen all day.'

'How much do I owe you for your time?'

'Ten minutes' work? On the client's site.' She scratched her chin, making a mock calculation. 'That'll be twenty five quid, plus travel.'

Jack inhaled deeply. 'I should've enquired beforehand.' He wiped his brow, calculating. 'Do you really charge £150 an hour?'

'My firm does.'

He shook his head. 'Wow. You're not getting near my accounts. Unless you can do them in half an hour.'

'What's your turnover?'

'Sixty thou last year, including materials and transport...'

She flapped a dismissive hand. 'Far too fiddly. Can't be bothered with boxes of screws and jars of nails.'

'Same principle,' he said, a little hurt at the dismissal of his turnover.

'I'm no cheap-jack.' She grinned.

'I most definitely am,' he said. 'Which is why I am here. Jack of All Trades.'

'Is that your van outside?'

'It is.'

'Well, I've remembered it,' she said. 'Can't say it's the best strapline in the world.'

'That's why I can't afford your fee.' He shrugged. 'You stay here much?'

'I do three days here and two in Sheffield. I've a house there. I'm thinking of moving down...but there's some uncertainty at the firm. I'll decide in a few months.'

'I'll give you a reference for your maths,' he said. 'How's your astronomy?'

'I know how to find the Pole Star. I can recognise the moon. There are nine planets, no, eight, Pluto has been demoted. How does it go?' She bit her lip and then exclaimed triumphantly as she reeled off the mnemonic, 'My Very Educated Mother Just Served Us Nine Pizzas.'

'That still has Pluto,' he said.

'For old time's sake,' she said. 'They had no right demoting it. I am sure it was devastated. Goes every week to Orion for counselling.'

'I've a telescope,' he said. 'Should be a clear night tonight. Might just catch Orion in the west.'

He was looking up at the sky, wondering whether she'd come out on the Flats with him with his telescope. She hadn't mentioned a husband or partner... So maybe. But £150 an hour? Could be way beyond his pocket.

Jack hesitated too long. A call came from the French windows. Cleo was standing there, waving her arms.

'Breakfast!'

Chapter 2

Five, including Jack, were seated at the table in the lounge with Cleo running to and fro from the kitchen. Eggs, bacon and beans, she placed out on heated trays in the centre with a large plate of toast. Jack had a coffee and a small plate by him. Tentatively, he took a slice of toast. The other items weren't for him, unless invited, although he could murder some bacon. But he knew the rules. He wasn't a paying guest.

Of the other four, the only one he knew was Beryl. Opposite him was a portly, middle aged black man, definitely familiar. A former customer maybe? He had a shaven head, making baldness a statement, rather than pretending with a comb-over. He was wearing a smart grey suit with a red tie.

Beryl was seated next to the man. She had helped herself to a couple of fried eggs and bacon.

'You know you snore, Clyde?' she said, addressing the man.

'I'm sorry,' said Clyde. 'I got a little drunk last night. It's been a stressful week.'

'A little!' she exclaimed. 'You were utterly out of it. I tried to wake you twice to turn off the roar. No chance.'

'Sorry.'

'I didn't sleep a wink,' she said. 'And I've a full day's work ahead.'

'I won't drink tonight,' he said, his eyes on his plate. 'I had a terrible flight over. And what with one thing and another...' He flapped a hand to stop himself. 'No excuses. I know I make a racket, but it's only when I'm drunk.' He turned to Beryl. 'Please accept my apology.'

'Not a lot else I can do,' she said coldly.

The outburst had quietened everyone. The man sitting by Jack was a middle aged white man, also in a suit, making Jack feel out of place in this company. The man was slim, his face pinkish, Jack could smell his aftershave. His hair was receding and he'd gone for the comb-over. Jack wondered how long he had himself before he would consider his options. Two bays were inching into his scalp, hidden by his curly hair, but not for much longer.

Everyone was shower fresh and well dressed including another black man at the end of the table, who was in smart casual wear, a green polo neck shirt and beige chinos. His hair was short, tight to his head, with no sign of loss. Although middle aged, he might have been an athlete in his younger years with his sleek body. He had a missing centre tooth which was difficult not to look at as he spoke.

Jack had washed in the patio tap, but hadn't taken off his boots or overalls. Not that taking them off would have fitted him in, as his jeans were well past their wash-by date.

Cleo brought in a large pot of tea and joined them at the free end of the table by Jack.

'For those of you who don't know,' she said, touching him on the shoulder, 'this is Jack, who is building my shed. Except I shall call it my summerhouse. Definitely bijou and upmarket.'

'How about dacha then?' said the black man with the missing front tooth.

'I like that, George. Unique for Forest Gate.'

'A shed by any other name,' said Beryl primly, 'is still a shed.'

Cleo pursed her lips, but did not reply.

'What are you going to do with it?' said the white man with the comb-over.

'Well, Larry, it will be my studio. I need somewhere to paint and do my mosaics. And I'll keep a futon there for when the house is full.'

'Is that legal?' said Larry.

'I won't let it out,' she said. 'It's like having a tent in the garden. It will be my backup.'

Jack had his eye on the last two rashers on the hot plate. If no one wanted them... Then George took one and Beryl the other. Never mind. He stretched for the marmalade and spread it on a slice of toast. Tomorrow, he'd have his coffee outside. It was uncomfortable watching the others eat a full breakfast.

'Jack has a telescope,' said Beryl.

'Oh really,' said Larry. 'Is it a big one?'

'Medium,' said Jack, taking a sip of coffee. 'A 150 Newtonian reflector.'

'What's that in English?'

Jack was on home ground, happy to elaborate on his pastime. 'It's a reflector because it has a mirror instead of a lens. 150 millimetres is the diameter of the mirror, 6 inches in imperial. The bigger the mirror, the more light you get in, the more you can see in the night sky.'

'And Newtonian?' asked Larry as he poured himself a cup of tea.

'There are different reflectors,' he said. 'The Newtonian was the first one, invented by Isaac Newton.' It was as if he were reading from one of his astronomy mags. And in a way he was, eager when the mag arrived to read the articles for new kit. 'The Newtonian is rather cumbersome, so that's why the others were invented.' He held up his hands, aware he was speaking too much. 'I don't want to take over the conversation. Telescope talk gets technical.'

'You could bring it over this evening,' suggested Cleo. 'Set it up in the garden.' She clapped her hands. 'Yes! We'll have a stargazing barbecue.'

11

'I could,' he said with reluctance. Too late to ask Beryl out anyway. Look willing, everyone was waiting for him. 'It's going to be a clear night. So why not?'

'Wonderful,' exclaimed Cleo. 'We eat at seven.'

'I'll be here,' he said.

'Have the last egg, Jack.'

'No, really. It's OK.' He recognised it as a reward for coming over tonight with his telescope. And didn't wish to be bought by a runny egg.

'Have it,' Cleo insisted. And when he hesitated, she gathered up the fried egg with a slice and put it on his plate. 'I know you builders need feeding.'

'Thanks,' said Jack. He dipped a bit of toast into the fried egg, and ate it with tea. It was there, why fight it? And his evening was taken care of. It was only up the road and he'd get fed too. And perhaps a second chance with Beryl.

'So what's everyone doing today?' enquired Cleo, looking around the table as if these were her children.

'The office, the office, same as always,' said Beryl with a yawn, perhaps at the thought of the office, perhaps for Clyde's benefit.

And £150 an hour, thought Jack.

'I'm sightseeing,' said Clyde. 'The British Museum, I think. What's the easiest way there?'

'Forest Gate station to Stratford,' said Cleo. 'Then change for the Central Line, to Holborn. It's a ten minute walk from there.'

'Thank you,' said Clyde.

'I was thinking of going there myself,' said George. Jack had to look down at his plate to not gaze at the missing centre tooth as he spoke. 'We could team up.'

'I've things to do first,' said Clyde hurriedly. 'The bank, some phone calls, a personal visit.'

It was obvious Clyde was pushing him away.

'We could go later then,' said George. 'Early afternoon.'

'I can't fix a timetable,' said Clyde. 'Maybe I'll see you there.'

Jack doubted it.

'How about you, Larry? Office?'

'That was the plan,' he said. 'But I got a phone call about quarter of an hour ago: the client has cancelled. I've a day off. I was wondering...' He looked to Jack. 'I might give you a hand. I've done a fair bit of DIY.' He added hesitantly, 'That's if it's OK with you.'

Jack considered whether having a mate would be more trouble than he was worth.

'You're not dressed for it,' he said.

'No,' Larry admitted, 'I didn't come prepared for manual work.'

'I've some overalls,' exclaimed Cleo. 'Baggy on me. Fit you fine.'

Jack considered saying No. He'd been in these situations before. Could be an awful chore. First telling them what to do, watching them do it badly, then correcting their mistakes. But there was Cleo, his client, egging him on.

The table was waiting on him.

'OK,' said Jack. 'But you can't wear those shoes. Got any others?'

'I've a pair of trainers.'

Jack twisted his nose in disapproval. 'All right, but at your own risk. I'm not insured for you.'

'At my own risk, boss.'

Jack thought of the job. It might work out. There was digging to do, and he'd had those dizzy spells. Maybe Larry could dig. He had volunteered after all. Give him the heavy work. He might enjoy it.

'And you, George?' said Cleo.

Jack wondered whether she did this every morning, making sure everyone was occupied.

13

'British Museum, maybe National Gallery.' Jack wondered at his age, late thirties, early forties. On his own, seeing the sights. 'I've a spare ticket for Les Mis tomorrow night. I was thinking of offering it to you, Beryl.'

'It's been on forever,' she said with a flap of the hand. 'Seen it and the movie. Even read half the book.'

'I was in it,' said Cleo, mock primly.

'Really?' said Beryl.

'Early 90s. Just the chorus. If I wasn't eating I'd give you a tap dance. I wonder if anyone I knew is still there. They'd be bored sick of it by now.'

'I didn't know you were an actress,' said Larry.

'Actor,' she corrected him. 'I went to the Italia Conti acting school. I was all set up to be a star. Up there with Judy Garland.' She sang to the ceiling, '*Somewhere over the rainbow, way up high...* It started fine. I got Les Mis only a few weeks out of school. Great time. I was fine with parts in the chorus. Then I began to get bigger roles in plays and musicals. And I got stage fright. Awful. Uncontrollable.' Her hands went to her cheeks as if reliving the horror. 'I'd be in the wings waiting to go on, trembling with fear. It got to the point when I couldn't sleep, so anxious for the next day. I tried hypnotherapy, counselling, yoga. Nothing worked. So here I am, everyone, running a B & B in Forest Gate.'

'You're still a star with us,' said George.

'Thank you, oh so much,' she beamed. 'I shall take three curtain calls.'

Jack turned to Clyde. 'I know you from somewhere.'

'I doubt it,' he said. 'I've been abroad for years.'

'You're so like someone I knew from Cumberland school.' He snapped his fingers. 'Paul! Paul Blake.'

'Not me. Never been anywhere near Cumberland school.'

'I went there,' piped up George. He turned to Jack. 'I thought I recognised you. What's your name now?' He flicked his fingers. 'Can't remember.'

Jack peered at him. 'I'm Jack Bell. Do I know you?' He put down his fork. 'When did you lose that tooth?'

'Playing football,' said George, 'but that was after I'd left school. So that won't help you.'

'I'm good at faces,' said Jack. 'But I haven't got you.'

'George Francis. And I know your sort,' he said, a little peeved. 'One of those guys can't tell one black from another.'

'It's early in the day,' said Jack, not rising to the taunt. 'And more than twenty years ago. Give me a break. So, what you up to these days?'

'I'm in IT,' said George. 'I live and work out in Southend. Got a few days off and I thought I'd have a look at the old haunts. Saw this place on TripAdvisor...'

The front door opened and slammed hard. All eyes turned to the hallway.

'Hello?' called out Cleo. 'Who's there?'

'It's me, Mum,' came a male voice. 'I'm back.'

Chapter 3

Cleo and her son, Martin, were in the kitchen, the detritus of cooking on the stove, worktops and table, the dishwasher wide open. She'd drawn him into there at once, away from the breakfast crowd. She closed the door and exploded.

'Two years!' she exclaimed. 'And not a word. Then you turn up out of the blue.' She imitated him with sarcasm, 'It's me, Mum. I'm back!' She shook her hands as if itching to strangle him. 'Not a phone call, not an email. How can you do this!'

Martin's hair was an untidy bush, he was darker than his mother. His jeans were torn, his top a dirty yellow with Bob Marley's head in black. His trainers had no laces.

'It's been difficult,' he said with a shrug. 'I had my phone and gear stolen.'

'No phone for two years, huh? Out in the desert so no internet connection.' She sighed heavily. 'Would it have been so difficult to borrow a phone? Pop into an internet café wherever you were.' Cleo flapped her hands wildly. 'And then you just turn up, expecting me to throw my arms round you. Mum's always here, always obliging.' She clutched her head in exasperation. 'Where the hell have you been?'

'Everywhere.' He looked around the kitchen, sniffing. 'I'm famished. I'll tell you everything soon, but I haven't eaten since yesterday.'

'Sit down,' she ordered.

And pushed him into a chair. She rapidly buttered two slices of bread and slapped a piece of cheese in between.

She was going for a plate but he grabbed it from her and wolfed it.

'You are starving.'

'All my money went on the air ticket,' he said, his mouth full.

'Stop talking. Eat.' She poured some juice and handed it over. 'I hate you, you know, doing this to me again. Thinking just of yourself.'

'I had nowhere else to go, Mum.' He swigged the juice. 'How I needed that!'

Cleo was racing about the kitchen getting bits and pieces from shelves and the fridge. On a plate, she handed him a ham sandwich with mustard, tomato and lettuce.

'Eat this. Stay here! I've got to talk to my guests.' She was shaking, her hands in a frenzy, as if wondering what duty came first. She stopped by the door, closed her eyes and spoke slowly as if to some invisible presence. 'Breathe in. Feel the ground. The tips of my fingers, the clothes on my back, the hair on my head, the tongue in my mouth, breathe out.' She exhaled and opened her eyes. 'You still here? I was hoping...' She shook her head. 'I am pleased to see you, Martin. I'm glad you are home. Eat. The guests will be gone soon. We'll talk then.' She kissed him on the cheek. 'Let's hope it's better this time round.'

Chapter 4

Jack had returned from his van with a wheelbarrow containing two spades, his metre spirit level and a long plank hanging over the front. By the site was Larry in white, paint-splattered dungarees. He'd rolled up his white shirt sleeves, ready to go. Jack looked at his trainers, expensive Adidas. Fashion stuff. But Larry had offered.

'See this area?' Jack indicated the rectangle of lawn with the four pegs and the string round the perimeter. 'That's going to be the shed floor base. We've got to dig down 8 inches.'

'20 centimetres.'

Jack smiled. Quite impressed. Maybe not just a soft office dude. 'Just make sure it's not 20 inches.'

'I think you'd notice.'

'Then we level it.' He shook the spirit level as if it were a talisman. 'That's what this is for. Then we fill in. First 7 centimetres of hardcore. There's a cubic metre of it in the drive. Then 5 centimetres of sand. Level it. Then 8 centimetres of concrete on top to make a base that will last longer than you or I will.'

'How long for it to dry?'

'I'll leave it a week. I've got some roof work between. Then we assemble the summerhouse.' He grinned at the term. 'Posh word for a big shed.'

Larry smiled.

'Any good at digging?' enquired Jack looking at his trainers.

'Could do with boots,' said Larry, acknowledging the gaze. 'I've got an allotment back home.'

'That's what I like to hear,' said Jack. 'We've got to get the turf off first.' He placed the plank on the outside along the string line. Then took a spade from the wheelbarrow. 'We use the plank as an edge and go all the way round, slicing into the turf a few inches.' He demonstrated, standing on the plank, and pushing the spade into the soil against the edge, moving on and doing the same, cutting a straight line. 'All the way round the perimeter,' said Jack. 'I'll leave you with that, OK?'

'No problem,' said Larry. 'I'll get on with it.'

Jack watched him start. Larry stepped on the plank and cut in against its edge.

'That's the way,' he said. 'All the way round the edge, keep it straight. Don't rush. I'll bring in the gear.'

Jack emptied the wheelbarrow and headed across the lawn to the patio. The turf was softish as there'd been quite a bit of rain recently. He'd given Larry a simple enough task, and he looked comfortable with it, which saved Jack from the unpleasant task of sending him packing. Larry looked somewhat doleful though. Something was troubling the man; life not right at home perhaps.

It was odd too, getting a day off because someone cancelled. There must be other things he could be doing at work. Jack shrugged. Not his business why Larry wanted the day off. He wasn't paying him, and if Larry wanted to give a hand, why discourage him?

Jack wheeled the barrow down the passage between the house and fence. The kitchen window was open and he could hear Cleo's raised voice. Curious, he stopped just past the window.

'Out of the blue,' she exclaimed. 'Two years. You could have been dead for all I knew. Then you turn up like a bad penny. I don't know where I'm going to put you. The house is full.'

He'd heard enough and pushed on. Family aggro and a full house. Poor Cleo, snoring guests and then her son turns up. He'd only glimpsed the young man before Cleo had rushed him away. Black, a bush of hair and slim as a rake. What had he been doing for two years? He thought of his daughter Mia, and why some couples didn't want children. Years of upbringing and then the problems they drop in your lap. How old was her son, early twenties perhaps? She'd been worrying about him for two years, utterly helpless.

Not that Jack had been the best of sons himself. He hadn't seen his father in four years and didn't miss him much. His mother lived in Plaistow; he went to see her about every six weeks, usually with Mia. Should he try to find his dad? He'd run off with a woman he was working with. Maybe he had a new family.

Though it was a double-sided coin. His dad could contact him; he wasn't exactly invisible.

Happy families are fine. When they're not happy, there's the hassle. Cleo didn't want to yell at her son, he didn't want to be yelled at. He thought of his mum and dad, the yelling before he'd left them. Jack thought of Alison, his ex, that period three years ago, seemed to be one big harangue, broken up by drunken episodes. Temper, territory. How can anyone believe we are not naked apes?

Jack had come outside with the wheelbarrow. At the side of the drive was the cement mixer, a cubic metre of hardcore in a large open sack, ditto of sand, and bags of cement. None of it was needed for a while; the site had to be dug out before anything could go in. He'd come out to leave Larry to it, so he wouldn't be standing over him. The fact was, he had some anxiety about the doctor's appointment. He'd been pushing it aside. It was routine. It was nothing.

20

Though why would the doctor call him in, unless something had shown up in the blood test results?

No point worrying, but that never stopped anyone. He'd give Larry five minutes or so. Either he'd be getting on with it or making a royal mess of things. Jack looked down the road. It was his road, just a few minutes to his house, along the tree-lined street. Leaves just coming on the plane trees, birds singing, though he could rarely spot them in the trees and didn't know what they were beyond pigeons and black-birds.

His phone rang. Alison, his ex.

'Hello,' he said. 'What can I do for you?'

'You busy?' she enquired.

'You got work for me?'

'No. I'm being sociable. I've got a team meeting after school, then a parents' evening. Who'd be a headteacher! Can you have Mia tonight?'

'Let me just check my busy social calendar with my secretary. You are so lucky, I have a gap tonight.' He could take his daughter to the barbecue. But he held back on saying that to Alison. She'd go on about homework, music practice, or something or other.

'I'll count myself one of the fortunate few,' she said. 'So you have Mia. That's one problem solved. It's a war zone here.'

'No time for love life?'

'As it happens, I am seeing someone.' She hesitated. 'But...'

'Too posh for you?'

'I'm getting fussy in my old age.'

'You're not forty!' He had to berate her; he was the same age. And was reminded of his doctor's appointment. Kill the thought. 'What's to be fussy about?'

'Do I really want to know the problems he's having with his father and sister?'

Or Jack's anxiety at the doctor's appointment. Busy head teacher, problem collector.

'Move on,' he said, almost adding there's plenty more fish in the sea, but they do seem to thin out as you age.

'I may just,' she said. 'But you know...' she sighed, 'at my time of life, do I really want to do more dating? It's such a strain, so time consuming.'

'You *are* old.' He couldn't help himself. 'It's a state of mind, they say.'

'So where does that leave you? Don't answer, Jack. Work to do,' she said. 'And I don't plan on dying just yet. I'll call Mia and tell her to go to your place after school. Thanks.' She hung up.

Jack sighed with relief. He hadn't mentioned his fears, and she hadn't criticised him. With Alison's phone calls, it was like being sent to the Head's office for some unknown reason. A relief to be off the hook. He hadn't seen Mia for a week, so it'd be good to catch up.

Jack laid the timber lengths on the wheelbarrow. It was to be the frame to hold the hardcore, sand and concrete. He headed back. Better see what Larry was up to. Passing the kitchen, he heard the young man mumbling to his mother. A précis of two years, no doubt. Why he'd been too busy to phone, his troubles, to add to Cleo's list.

Another agony aunt.

As he came off the alley, Jack watched Larry working. He seemed to be doing OK, going round the edge with the spade, standing on the board.

'What do we do with all the turf and soil, Jack?' he called, stopping as Jack came in.

'Cleo wants a rock garden. Over there.' Jack pointed to the far corner of the lawn. 'We dump all the turf and earth there. That's all we need to do. She can shape it and put the rocks in. Not our concern.' Jack lifted the timber off the wheelbarrow and placed it on the grass. 'Bit odd you getting a day off, if you don't mind me saying. Convenient for me, but I'd have thought there'd be other work for you to do.'

As he was saying it, he knew he should've shut up. Not his business. But it was said, and had silenced Larry. He was on the plank, the spade halted in the earth, stuck like a photo, allowing Jack to realise he'd been right about the oddity.

A few seconds passed, enabling Jack to guess what he was about to hear.

'There's no job, Jack,' Larry said at last. 'There hasn't been for two months.'

Jack took this in. It wasn't a confidence he wanted. But he had asked for it, and been told. Now he was committed to hearing the full tale. Big mouth.

'I assume your wife doesn't know,' he said. In for a penny, in for a pound.

Larry nodded. 'She thinks I'm working three days a week in London.' He gave a half laugh. 'I've been to every museum in town, seen the latest films, I could tell you every Starbucks in the West End.'

'Can you afford it?'

Larry shrugged. 'Maybe for another six months. I've got a cheap rate here. Beryl fixed it for me. You know she's my sister?'

'I didn't.'

'It's why I came here.' He wiped down his comb-over. 'I'm her big brother, though you wouldn't know it. She's the one got it all sussed.'

'Does she know you're not working?'

'I'm not sure,' he said. 'I have a feeling she suspects something is up. Don't know.' He shook his head. 'Stupid really, the whole thing. The longer it goes on, the harder it is to back down.'

Jack had to ask the obvious question.

'Why are you pretending?'

'Pride,' said Larry with a faint smile. 'My self image, for what it's worth. My wife is the accounts manager of a carpet firm. Earns more than I do.' He halted an instant and corrected himself. 'Than I did. No kids at home. A son studying in the States. So it's just the two of us facing each other across the table. She was promoted two months ago. She was over the moon, I'd just been fired. I couldn't tell her. Lost the opportunity.'

'Why were you fired?'

'I'd rather not say.'

'Fine.' Obviously something he wasn't proud of. Sexual harassment, stealing, watching porn, coming in drunk, insulting his boss or even hitting him. Any one of the above. Jack had heard the full list from recovering alcoholics at Alcohol Halt. Men were all the same, as Alison would tell him.

'Why are you telling me?' he said.

Larry sighed heavily. 'I couldn't face another museum. I got up this morning, put my suit on and suddenly realised I couldn't go on, saw you working out here...' He leaned on the spade. 'I envy you. The simplicity of manual work. Being your own boss.'

'It's no bed of roses,' said Jack. Then added, after a thought, 'Now you've told me, tell Beryl. Then your wife. You could say you'd been made redundant.'

'And then what? When I can't get another job.'

'Bad reference, you mean?' Larry nodded. 'You'll have to go for self employment. I did. I got sacked for being drunk in a warehouse. Once I'd got myself together, I realised it was the only way to go.'

'I was wondering if I could work with you.' He pulled the spade over his shoulder, like a soldier at drill.

Jack held up his hands, to hold off the request. 'I've only just met you, Larry. Nothing personal, but I prefer working alone.' He stopped, seeing Larry's downcast expression.

'Sorry, but I can't help you with work.' After a pause, he added, 'Sounds like your marriage is in a bad state.'

'It is.'

'Start there,' he said. 'Decide whether you want to save it or not.'

'Shouldn't drop this on you.' He gave a half smile. 'Thanks for listening. I'll carry on.'

Larry went back to cutting the edge. Jack picked up the other spade. He'd known something was up when Larry asked if he could work with him. A stranger volunteering, there had to be a reason, some screw-up in his life.

It's always easier to say no at the beginning.

And then he felt guilty. He'd been helped when he needed it, and was the person Larry had confided in. Don't judge, said Alcohol Halt. We're all idiots pretending we're not. Can't be argued with. Larry must be overspending to keep up his pretence. That had to stop. But did he want to get involved?

Advice was easy to give and mostly not welcome.

Shut up.

Jack started at an edge Larry had cut. With the blade end of his spade, he scored out a rough oblong of turf. There was no need for accuracy as they weren't going to be laid anywhere. He levered underneath it with the spade, rolling it, as the blade went through, like a piece of carpet. And he threw the turf length into the wheelbarrow.

'I don't mind talking about it, Larry,' he said. 'A sounding board, if you like. And it's fine to have you working with me today. But I can't offer you paid work. This job is too tight. I'll listen though, if it helps.'

Larry moved along the plank with his spade and pressed it into the turf.

'I appreciate that, Jack.'

Chapter 5

As Cleo came into the lounge, Clyde stood up from the sofa. He folded the newspaper he'd been reading, and put it on the coffee table.

Cleo said, 'Might I have a word?'

'I'm about to go out,' he said. He picked up a backpack.

'I'll only be a minute, Clyde. If you don't mind.'

He sat on the arm of the sofa and avoided her eye.

'I know what this is about,' he said.

'What?' she said.

Cleo was wearing an apron over her clothes with a flat cook's hat, her hair tucked under. She'd been busy in the kitchen, keeping the door shut as she cleared up breakfast and had it out with her son.

'Snoring,' he said. He crossed one leg awkwardly over the other. 'I've been told before. It's embarrassing. I hate it. I shouldn't drink. It's just I've had a lot on my mind, plus the journey. A ten hour flight.'

'I'm going to swap rooms with you,' she said. 'This isn't negotiable. Beryl is one of my regulars. I can't have her disturbed. Her brother Larry stays here too. I can't have ructions.'

'You want me to have your room?' he said. He was playing with the end of his red tie, spotted what his fingers were doing and stopped.

'Yes, I do.'

'That's not fair on you.'

'My problem,' she said. 'I'm used to it.'

Clyde took his phone from his pocket and glanced at the time. 'I can't move my things now. I'll be late. I have an important appointment.'

'I'll move you,' she said. 'I'll put everything in your suitcase and move it to my room. I'll make sure it's neat and tidy for you.'

'A move isn't necessary,' he said. 'I won't be drinking tonight.'

'I can't risk it,' she said. 'Not with Beryl. As I said, this is not negotiable, Clyde.'

'What's the alternative?'

She shrugged. 'It's obvious, really.'

'I leave?'

'I don't want you to go, Clyde, but there's limited space here. Let's keep it cool. My room is large, has an en-suite bathroom.' She smiled. 'Consider it an upgrade.'

He stood up, put the backpack on his back.

'OK,' he said. 'I caused the hassle, so it's best I move rooms. Sorry for the trouble.'

'Don't worry about that,' said Cleo. 'Do I have permission to move your stuff?'

'You do.'

'Thank you for being understanding,' she said. 'So be on your way. Don't forget we have the barbecue and telescope do tonight.'

'I'm looking forward to it.' He sighed. 'I'll be off the booze. Nothing but fizzy water.' He looked at his phone again. 'Must go, must go. Sorry to put you to the trouble.'

'I run a B & B,' said Cleo. 'Trouble is my middle name.'

Clyde left the room with a wave of his hand. When the front door had closed on him, Cleo collapsed onto the arm of the sofa. At least that was done with. Just her son to sort out. She looked about the sitting room. Not too untidy. She'd vacuum it once she'd moved Clyde. Get that over and done with. She glanced in the large mirror, seeing her hat and apron, and ripped them off; they were kitchen wear. Cleo went into the hallway and threw them in the tall Ali Baba basket.

Lots to do.

Move Clyde, change the sheets in his room and hers, vacuum, laundry, shopping. In her room, she'd have to put her things away in the big cupboard to leave it tidy for Clyde. Including the mosaic she was working on; such a pain to have to move it. Cleo had slept in every room in the house, except the kitchen and bathrooms. It went with the job. She accepted the inconvenience as a solution to keeping the bookings coming in.

One day, very soon, she'd have her summerhouse. Her art could stay put and she could sleep there from time to time and wake with the sun streaming in. Hard to imagine the day.

Cleo took the stairs two at a time. They were carpeted in pale grey, a thick pile. With a busy house, and guests coming in and out at all hours, it was essential to keep foot-fall on the stairs as quiet as possible.

Clyde's room was across the landing from the top of the stairs. She took the bunch of keys off her belt, knowing them all off by heart, the shape, the scratches. No need for colour codes. And she put the right one in the keyhole. She was surprised to find the door was not locked. Careless of Clyde. She always told guests to lock their rooms, she couldn't be responsible otherwise.

Cleo opened the door. There was George, by the side of the unmade bed.

'What are you doing here?' she demanded.

George held up his hands in surrender. 'This isn't what it seems,' he said.

'How did you get in?'

'It's a simple lock,' he said. 'Let me explain.'

'Empty your pockets,' she said, hands on hips.

'I haven't taken anything. Believe me.' He shook his hands back and forth as if to fend her off. 'That's not why I'm here.'

'Empty your pockets,' she said, taking a step towards him. When he hesitated, she added, 'Otherwise I'm calling the police.'

George hesitated for a second, then considered he was compromised enough and began emptying his pockets on to the duvet. A wallet, keys, a handkerchief.

'Put your arms in the air,' she said.

'What for?'

'Just do it. You shouldn't be in here. Do it.'

He raised his arms. Cleo came forward and patted him down, from his chest, his trousers, front pockets, back pocket. She stopped at the latter and took out a bit of paper. She looked at it.

'Two tickets for Les Mis,' she said.

'Satisfied?'

'No,' she said. 'You don't seem to have anything, so maybe I caught you in time.' She picked up his wallet and opened it. 'How do I know this money is yours?' She fingered a hundred pounds or so in notes.

'It's all mine,' he said. 'I swear. On my mother's life.'

'Mothers don't count for much today,' she said. She shook the notes in his face. 'I'm taking it,' and she pocketed the cash. 'When Clyde gets back, if he doesn't complain about stolen money, I'll return it.' She looked at the two credit cards in the wallet, his name on both. Then at a card in one of the pockets. It had a photo in the corner. She looked at George then back at the photo. The same deep brown face, short hair, though he had his mouth closed in the photo to hide the missing tooth. She read it carefully, then said, 'You're a private investigator.'

'I am,' he said.

'So why are you searching Clyde's room?'

'I've every reason to believe Clyde is a wanted criminal. He was involved in a multi million pound raid of safety deposit boxes. He has been out of the country for seventeen years...'

'Why aren't the police investigating this?'

He gave a gapped tooth smile. 'The police are incompetent. Or being paid off. And my client wants his property back.'

'They're willing to go through devious channels.'

'No, I am,' he said. 'My client needs proof of identification. I came in here to get a DNA sample.' He hesitated, then indicated the handkerchief on the bed. 'That's his. It's all I want. It'll have his DNA.' His eyes widened, pleading. 'Just the hankie, Cleo. That's all I need. He won't miss it.'

'No. You can't break into one of my guests' rooms and leave with loot. Not even a hankie.'

George scratched his chin, staring at the items on the bed. 'You can have the money, Cleo. There's a hundred in cash. Keep it. And I'll have the handkerchief.'

Cleo bit her thumb tip, considering the deal. She looked around the room. There wasn't much here. It was unlikely Clyde would have left anything valuable. It was a good offer.

'Two hundred,' she said.

'For a handkerchief! You must be joking.'

'You broke into Clyde's room, George. That's a criminal act.'

He squeezed his nose. She figured he was rapidly calculating income and expenditure as she would be.

'One fifty. That's my limit. Way over the top.'

Cleo nodded. 'I'll add the fifty to your bill,' she said. 'Take the hankie and get out.'

Chapter 6

'Please sit down, Mr Bell.'

Jack's doctor, Dr Aziz, was a slim, young Asian man, thirty at a stretch. His hair was short and black, his complexion a smooth brown. He probably cycles to work, thought Jack. The young doctor had the sleeves of his white shirt rolled up, giving the impression of efficiency.

'I'm looking at the results of your blood test, Jack.' He was looking at the laptop screen on his desk.

'I'm all ears,' said Jack, wondering what was to come.

He had left Larry to carry on with the digging, and had walked to the Lister Health Centre. It wasn't far, easier to walk than sort out parking. He was unlikely to be here long, anyway.

'In a nutshell,' Dr Aziz turned away from the screen, 'you have type 2 diabetes.'

That struck like a punch in the guts.

'That can't be possible,' he exclaimed. 'I'm barely forty.'

Aziz smiled. 'I have diabetic patients way younger than forty. Some in their teens.'

Jack wiped his brow with the back of his hand, taking in what the young doctor was telling him. What did it mean? Jobwise, personal life?

'Is it certain?'

'Your blood sugar is too high. It's either Pre or Early, Jack. I'd like another blood test for confirmation. But certainly the dizziness and high sugar in the blood all point to Type 2.'

'I knew something wasn't right,' he said, 'but I never thought diabetes. Will I have to have injections?'

'No.' He waved a hand to dismiss the suggestion. 'It's early days for you. I shall give you some medication. And send you for another blood test so we can get more information. Do you eat breakfast in the mornings?'

Jack bit his lip guiltily. 'Sometimes I dash out without eating, or maybe just a slice of toast and a cup of tea. You know how it is? Then have something around ten.'

'Let's start there. You must eat properly and regularly. When you do eat, what's typical for your ten o'clock break?'

'Egg, bacon, fried bread.' Even as he was saying it, he was hearing Alison's criticism of his fry ups.

'And for lunch?'

'Cheese sandwiches. They're quick. Or a fry up at the local café.' He knew it was junk food, but everyone ate it. All the builders he knew.

'Do you snack between meals?'

'A Mars bar, a cream cake...' He hesitated then said, 'It's all wrong, isn't it?'

'Not exactly a balanced diet. What about your evening meals?'

'Take-aways. Pizza, Chinese.' He flapped a hand. 'Don't tell me. It's all junk. I never thought I'd be here, talking about diabetes. I get lots of exercise with my job. I'm not overweight.'

'Do you cook at all?'

'Not a lot.'

'Fresh fruit, vegetables?'

'Not much.'

Dr Aziz looked at the screen. 'I see you had a period of alcoholism. Is that under control?'

'I don't drink at all now,' said Jack. 'I go to Alcohol Halt from time to time.'

'Good,' said Aziz. 'I'm sure you have gathered from my questions that it's your eating habits that have got you to this juncture. Boozing has a legacy too, along with the fry ups and take-aways. You know the five a day rule for fruit and veg?'

'I do.'

'It's not just for children, you know. I want to see you eating fruit and green vegetables, salads. Less bread and potatoes. No fry ups.'

'Not even a fried egg?'

'Have it boiled or poached. The principles are simple: you must cut back on fat, sugar and other carbs. Go for the blood test in the next couple of days. No food before the test. I suggest you go first thing, then you can have a healthy breakfast and go to work. Once the results are in, I'll call you back. Here's a pamphlet on diet.' He handed it over to Jack. 'It's commonsense stuff. Regular meals. Cut down the carbs, five a day for fruit and veg, no fry ups. You must learn to cook. Early onset diabetes is reversible but only with a decent diet.'

'What if I carry on eating like I am? Tell me the worst that can happen.'

Dr Aziz smiled wryly. 'Let's take it in steps, Jack. In a year or two, you'll need to have insulin injections. And in the longer term, you risk blindness, losing a limb, and you can say goodbye to working for a living. Certainly not as a builder. Once you get to that point, you're on the slide. You'll be gaining weight, watching TV all day long, if your eyesight is holding out. If you miss injections, skip meals, or keep eating junk, you could go into a coma. And die.'

Jack blew out his cheeks as Aziz gave the timeline, envisioning himself stuck at home, bored, watching quiz shows and antique auctions, ballooning, hassled by Social Security, fifty looking seventy...

'I get the picture,' he managed to say.

33

'Totally in your hands, Jack. One important piece of advice.' Dr Aziz waved a finger at him. 'Don't keep it a secret. Tell other people. Then you are more likely to do something about it.'

Chapter 7

Clyde was on the 330 bus making its slow way down Green Street. The road was colourful and busy, many sari shops with red, blue and green saris on elegant mannequins in decorous poses. Had there been so many when he left? It had been an Asian shopping street, but he'd forgotten how Asian.

Not many black people around, or whites for that matter. Racism was too easy. Looking for numbers. This street shouldn't bother him. No one was attacking him, looking at him.

Live and let live.

People stick together, religion and culture. His family had ended up in Newham, it was cheap, they knew people here, got housed by the Council. A lot of racism on the estate and on the streets. All too easy, sinking back to easy judgements.

Having joined the middle class, it was too easy to forget where he'd come from.

Seventeen years away. This street was like a town in a city. Like drew in like, as it did in Vancouver. It was his job to be aware of such things. A realtor, an estate agent as they say here, at home. Whatever that means.

His clients were often racist. The way it was said; where they didn't want to live. The schools. People like us.

He'd been called a coconut once. Sucking up to well off white clients, absorbing their values as he nodded. Memory fades like the sun on dyed cloth, connections fall away. His boss had pushed him onto racist clients. He suspected deliberately. If he could have, he'd have left, but kids, the mortgage. He needed the job, so nod, agree, go along with them.

Until, little by little, you become a coconut. More white than black.

Jack Bell had recognised him. Clyde had denied knowing him, but he doubted Jack believed him. And George was watching him. Up to something without a doubt. Saying he was at the school too. A lie, he was sure of it.

He had been told not to come back. Stay in Canada. But Clyde had always been stubborn. A risk taker, which made it sound a virtue. Here and now, he doubted that. Was it rather a cowardice, a failure to face things? A hope in benign providence, which had lately deserted him.

The universe had it in for him. Stupid thought. It was a lottery, life.

The long flight over gave him too much time to think. It was foolhardy coming back. A few hours into the flight, he wanted to get off. But he couldn't parachute out into eastern Canada or over the Atlantic ocean. At Heathrow, it didn't seem so bad. A low level risk, until he got to Forest Gate and the fears crowded in. So he drank in his room, sloshing it back to kill thought. It knocked him out, and had him snoring like a goods train. That was so humiliating. First Beryl berating him in front of everyone at breakfast, then Cleo dressing him down like a schoolboy. Swap rooms or leave. How did she put it? It was non negotiable.

Perhaps he should leave the place. Quietly pack his suitcase this afternoon and sneak out. Then book into an anonymous hotel in Stratford. What had made him think a B & B would be better? People to talk to, sure, but now he saw that was the wrong idea. People ask questions; they might recognise him. He must cut back visibility, not court it. He should imprison himself in his room, watch TV.

But then he'd drink. Alone, of course he would. Drink into insensibility, wet the bed, snore the house down. Too easy to rabbit on with any stranger, so few brain cells functioning, he could blurt it all out. In vino, the idiot. Loving everyone, telling the deepest secrets, with complete trust in human beneficence.

The bus had halted at a bus stop. Passengers got on and off. Clyde was lost for a moment, where was he? This was familiar but not quite right. Then it filtered into place. This was where West Ham football team played, the Boleyn ground. But the ground had gone. Had become flats. Where had the team gone?

As a kid it had been a place to avoid on match day. Anyone black was in danger from the racists who seemed to have taken over the Hammers. In the 90s, it petered out with the all-seater ground and more black players. But he'd never gone.

It had hurt for a week being called a coconut.

At the corner by the Barking Road, there was the Boleyn pub. Or rather, what had been the Boleyn. Was it a wine bar? Not the spit and sawdust Boleyn, surely? Named after Anne Boleyn, he remembered from school. Henry VIII hunted round here, maybe took her along, until he chopped her head off.

If he himself had the power, what heads would roll?

Clyde culled the thought. He didn't have the power, doubtless it would make him a bastard too. But he was powerless, here with himself. His failure.

As the bus waited at the lights, he recognised the statues of the West Ham players who'd played in the England team that won the World Cup in '66. There was Bobby Moore, Martin Peters who got the hat trick. Who were the other two?

He couldn't remember. But he'd never been much of a West Ham supporter. He'd preferred Arsenal, no bad associations plus Thierry Henry, smart, black Frenchman and as skilful as they come.

The bus swung round onto the Barking Road, past the triumphant football players, heading west towards Plaistow. It looked much the same, this stretch. The small shops, the squat houses. They didn't seem small when he was a young-ster but his house in Vancouver with Susie and the kids was detached and twice the width. More.

There was the cash 'n' carry where he'd almost got caught shoplifting. He'd legged it with the Asian shopkeeper screaming after him. All for a few batteries, but for months afterwards he'd take a wide sweep round the shop, in case he was recognised.

His mate Barry had been first with a phone, one of those hefty things that were almost like a cosh in your hand. All the rage though, everyone wanted one. He wondered what Barry was up to now. Last he'd heard, more than seventeen years out of date, he was in with a drugs gang. Maybe just as well, he himself had gone away.

Where would he be if he hadn't? Dead? In the nick.

He alighted at the corner of Prince Regent Lane, and walked up the hill to where the sewerbank met the road. There was a wrought iron archway, on the top, he couldn't believe it, it said Greenway. Everyone knew huge sewer pipes passed under the road, across and down the wide strip that ran all the way down to Beckton sewage works. Every few hundred yards there was a vent where you caught a whiff of the sludge running through.

Greenway! The realtor in him loved it. It was green, he could agree to that. The pipes were earthed over and grassed. But it was the underneath, the not-so-secret secret, the real purpose. North London's slurry heading for the toilet.

He walked on smiling at the rebranding. There was NewVic, he remembered that, new in his day, a college now, but his old school used to be there, Cumberland. Where he, Jack and George had resisted the state's attempts to educate them. Though a little had stuck in his case, in spite of everything. To his surprise, he was chosen to play Banquo in Macbeth. Half the cast were black too, that was the school. But the language in the play, so twisted, so hidden. And having to learn it. Still, it was sharp, he had to admit, when he got the hang of it. He got killed fairly early on, by Macbeth's heavies, but had to come back as a ghost at the feast to haunt Macbeth.

He might as well be a ghost now. Felt like one, in these half remembered streets. The things that had made him. He was still the Plaistow boy with his bad dreams.

Clyde turned into the road that led to the hospital. Newham General as was, now Newham University Hospital upgraded. He'd come here with a broken leg, Barry with a broken arm. The two of them on a bicycle with brakes so poor they were for decoration only. They'd come racing down a hill and couldn't stop at the lights, and smashed into the side of a cement lorry. Lucky to get off with just broken bones.

A black woman was coming towards him. It had to be Dido. He'd seen photos of her, knew she'd grown, but she was much bigger in the flesh. There was a whole lot of her. She waved, he waved back. He was no lightweight himself. The Plaistow boy had filled out.

She stopped and waited for him to come to her. A couple of yards away they stared at each other, each seeing themselves in the other. Such changes. She rushed forwards and embraced him. Her arms enfolding him, tears welling, he clutched her back, a ball of family.

'So good to see you, Dido,' he murmured, 'so good.'

'My little brother is as big as me,' she said laughing, looking him in the face, patting his cheeks. 'It's really you.'

'I think so,' he said.

They were both gazing at the body in front of them, wiping away the flesh they'd added. He saw her twenty years ago, in tottery high heels and a short skirt hobbling off to a Hackney club. Coming back in the early hours to be harangued by their mother.

Dido said, 'You shouldn't have come.'

'I've been thinking of it for years. And when you told me she was dying, last chance, I thought.'

She embraced him again.

'Clyde, Clyde, you are so big. You were a football player, not a sumo wrestler.'

'Size is in the family,' he said. And they both laughed.

Her hair was in neat Afro plaits, suiting her. She was wearing a colourful dress, tight about her full bosom. So like Mum when he was a kid. Dido's teeth were in good shape, very white, a test of how someone was doing when they came into his office. Good dental work was a sign of affluence.

'Who else is here?' he asked.

'Bobby. Auntie Beth, Uncle Joe, the cousins, everyone's been coming and going... They'll be so pleased to see you.' She shook her head sadly. 'But be prepared. Mum won't know you.'

'Is she that far gone?'

'I'm afraid so.' She took his arm. 'Come on. A day or two, that's all she's got. Heavily sedated. Let's get to the ward, little brother, before she passes on.'

Chapter 8

When Jack arrived back at Cleo's, after the heavy at the clinic, there was Larry with a coffee seated by the site on a patio chair, his legs splayed out. The turf had been cleared from the area, and he had begun the digging.

'Going well,' said Jack, impressed. 'Maybe I should head off to the pictures, leave you to it.'

'I'm shattered,' declared Larry. He wiped his brow with a tissue and slipped down in the chair to emphasise.

Jack had been away for at least an hour. There'd been the wait at the surgery, the appointment itself, and then he'd gone, with a prescription, to a nearby pharmacy. And waited there for it to be dispensed.

'Turf is heavy,' said Larry, his hands massaging his sides. 'A back breaker.'

'Don't kill yourself,' said Jack. 'You rest a while.'

Jack took a spade and began digging where Larry had left off. He was pleased with his assistant's work, Larry had been keeping to the eight inch depth, just short of a spade length. Not that it had to be accurate, as hard core and sand were to go on top. That would take out any unevenness.

'How did it go at the quack's?' said Larry.

Jack hesitated. Tell people, ordered Dr Aziz. Did he really want to tell all and sundry his troubles? It was Alcohol Halt's advice too. Secrets kill.

'I've got type 2 diabetes,' he said.

'Never!' exclaimed Larry. 'You're too young, you're not overweight, you get plenty of exercise... as I know to my cost.'

'Too much junk food,' he said. 'I've had an alcohol problem...'

'Well I never,' said Larry, looking Jack up and down. 'You're too fit, a picture of health...'

'I've had dizzy spells.'

Jack threw a spadeful of earth into the wheelbarrow as if to contradict his words. And in one movement, he brought the spade back to where he was digging, pressing it down with his boot and easing up another spadeful.

'Should you be doing this?' said Larry watching him dig. 'I don't want to get funny, but this is heavy work...'

'My thoughts exactly,' said Jack. 'But I don't want to be an invalid.'

'One doesn't always get the choice,' said Larry.

'But I have. So says the doctor. The remedy is simple, the man says. Eat regularly, eat well. Take the medicine. And with luck, the condition could reverse.' He shrugged, 'And if not, it can be contained.'

'And you can carry on working?'

'I hope so. I really hope so. I've been thinking about it,' he said. Non stop, he might have added, since he'd left the surgery. 'It's a question of thinking ahead. Be canny. Work steadily, take breaks, eat regularly. See? I know it already.'

'You could take someone on.'

That had occurred to Jack too, much as he preferred to work on his own. It was a consideration. But he didn't want to talk it with Larry angling for employment. If, a big if, he took someone on, then he'd want someone younger who could do the heavy work. He'd train them, that would be the deal. Larry was exhausted already.

'A possibility,' he said, as if it were the vaguest of thoughts.

They didn't speak for a minute. Jack worked on with the digging. He guessed Larry was considering whether he had a chance. And Jack didn't want to give any hint. He had enough on his plate.

'I'll get you a coffee,' said Larry, breaking the silence. He rose.

'No cake,' said Jack reluctantly. 'No biscuits.'

'I get the idea.'

Larry left him and crossed the lawn.

Jack continued digging, filling the wheelbarrow with soil. Work and take breaks. Eat. Don't take risks. Employ people? He was reminded of a scaffolder he knew. Hadn't seen him for a few years. Tom something or other. He had done well in the boom. Had taken his risks and had his own firm, two lorries, employed a dozen workers, wore a suit, posh watch, clean hands, pink nails. Then came the bust, big firms collapsing and dragging down myriad small fry with them. One of them was Tom's. The last he'd seen of him, he was a scaffolder again. Aged 55, a twelve foot metal pole across his shoulder, tiredness and loss etched into his forehead.

What a game!

Jack was younger, but it was as if today someone had jumped out of a hedge and handed him a 15 years older card. Instant ageing. His body failing him. He'd expected to slip gently into middle age, and over twenty, thirty years to old age. Gradual was the way he'd seen it. A long, easy slope. Not a sudden leap.

This was betrayal.

By whom exactly?

By the alcoholic, by the junk food junky. Not by him at all.

Jack threw another spadeful into the wheelbarrow. That would do. It wasn't full, could take more, but he had aged 15 years.

Stupidity.

Self pity. Banish it, said Alcohol Halt. A useless emotion. He wasn't dying. Dr Aziz had told him it was in his own hands. Jack pushed the wheelbarrow across the grass steadily, to fit his new age, to the far end of the lawn. There was a heap, mostly turfs, lying over each other like mating caterpillars. He tipped soil from the wheelbarrow on top.

Did he have the will power?

The drunk in him laughed outrageously, putting a hand on Jack's shoulder, telling him to live for the day. To hell with tomorrow.

The sober man in him said, today is tomorrow. Wise up.

'Jack!'

He looked across. Larry was at the patio table with a tray. Jack left the barrow and crossed over. On the table was a mug of coffee with a plate of salad. It was colourful with the tomato, lettuce, spring onions and celery.

But not very filling.

Chapter 9

Cleo was irritated. There were too many people about the house. Mostly during the day, she had the place to herself. But today, there was the builder and Larry working with him. That sudden day off didn't sound right, but none of her business. And then Martin swans in, as if he'd just been away for a weekend with friends.

She was up the ladder, climbing into the loft. Martin was below her, another vexation in her day. She would like to send him out shopping to get food for tonight's barbecue but feared he'd spend it on drink or drugs. He arrived on her doorstep without a penny in his pocket. Can you believe it? Would he get a job, or would he laze around all day? She'd ranted too much already. Shouting never worked; it just made him angrier, she more frustrated and desperate.

An intractable problem, expecting her to drop everything and cater for his needs, as if he were a babe in arms. You are an adult, she wanted to yell at him. Instead, she crawled into the loft and turned on the light. It was a low space without windows. You could just about stand up in the middle, but had to crawl at the eaves, and so it was only used for storage. Which was why she was up here. Martin had clothes stored up here, and other bits and pieces, but clothes were the priority; he couldn't stay here in that dirty gear. This was a business, she had standards. She'd leave him to sort out clothing; there were black bags of them thrust into the eaves. But she was here too for the tent and sleeping bag; which she'd seen in her last foray in the roof space.

Half the stuff could be thrown out. You think it might be useful, so put it in the loft. Years pass and it never is, you forget about it and push more boxes, pictures, broken chairs that could be repaired, toys, electronic stuff that nobody wants but is too good to throw out. What is good, what is junk in this throwaway world? Herself, she lived minimally. Running a bed and breakfast, frequently giving up her room meant she couldn't be a hoarder. Her one exception was her art. Art, and materials for art, accumulated, but clothing she would wear and wash until they fell to bits. Fashion wasn't for her. Utility was, unless you were speaking of art, when all bets were off. That's why she needed the summerhouse. Space, storage, light.

To hell with Martin. Her time was precious, the day too short, and then he's here, demanding she drop everything and serve him.

'Catch!' she shouted as she threw down the sleeping bag.

Conveniently it was by the tent. Some logic in the chaos. And the tent pegs too! She passed them down to Martin, working to hold off a sneeze. The dust. The sneeze overtook her, one then another, a fierce blast as if of frustration. She would be sneezing for an hour now. It got up her nose, made her eyes water.

She clambered down the ladder.

'Put the tent up right now,' she said.

'I need some clothes,' said Martin. 'There's plenty up there.'

'Put the tent up,' she insisted. 'Then you'll have somewhere to put your clothes.'

Martin would have rejected her suggestion, his default, but her back was to the ladder barring him from it. A challenge of the stubborn. She was adamant, knowing what would happen if she let him get the clothes first. He would dump them in the lounge. And there they would stay, amidst her frustration and yelling, until in a temper she would bin them.

She would not be his skivvy, though she could sense she already was. He could've got the tent himself, though he'd be asking her half a dozen times where it was.

It was all happening again, as if he'd never been away.

She never should have been a mother. Briefly married to a Ghanaian dancer who had two-stepped down to Australia, via West Africa, with a chorus girl from Sydney, leaving Cleo with the bump that would be Martin. Where Akip was now she had no idea, and didn't care. It had been lust, a pretend love. He was handsome, muscular, ebony smooth – and didn't he know it. As graceful as a gazelle as he glided from bed to bed.

Goodbye, good riddance, black dancer.

She was curious, though not caring, how he'd fared. Time's ravages. But a photo would serve, rather than his presence. She would be disappointed perhaps. Saddened even. Beauty is ephemeral. She'd been a looker herself. And now, holding on, with no time for such thoughts. Cleo pushed the ladder up, into its slide-away which closed the trap door to the loft.

The decision was made for Martin. He stared at her with hatred. She stared back.

'Two years,' she said, 'and not a word.'

Tight lipped, Martin picked up the tent and sleeping bag. And headed downstairs. She watched his retreating back. And sneezed twice, and by the time she looked again, he was out of sight, but she could hear his tread in the downstairs hallway, on the way to the garden.

Cleo wondered how long he'd stay. He was penniless, so no choice but to stay a while. She was his pad, his meal ticket. He'd told her a tale about working in a bar in Caracas, which might be true, although she suspected his employment had been less than legal as genuine work had never been Martin's penchant.

'Why have you no money or clothing?' she'd asked.

He'd said that he had crossed a gang boss, so had to leave in a mad rush. That had the ring of truth. Martin had criminal tendencies but he wasn't very good at it.

Oh! She hadn't been a bad mother, but her son's teenage years had abraded her sympathy. Drugs, arrests, gang wars, two stints in prison. The last time he came out he'd stolen her credit card, and maxed it out.

How much could she give him to go? Leave her in peace.

And then she'd suffer again.

He was part of her. She had been distressed when he hadn't communicated. Lying awake with worry in the early hours, anxious for little Martin when he was two and had whooping cough. She was his stone anchor, he knew it, could use it, ever would. Some time or other Martin would get a long stretch, here or in a foreign jail. She would visit, send parcels. She was damned to be his mother.

Cleo sneezed. And again, and a third time. Unlucky. She wiped her eyes with the back of her hand and listened. She was the only one in the house. Jack and Larry were working, Martin was in the garden attempting to put up the tent. An IQ test for his drug addled brain. She went to the linen cupboard and took out a bath and a hand towel. And went to George's room.

When she'd caught him in Clyde's room, he'd said he was a private eye. She had checked out the website on his card – and it seemed genuine. Though, whether his reason for being in Clyde's room was true, that was another matter.

Being Martin's mother had made her unremittingly suspicious.

Cleo closed the door behind her. The room was basic: a double bed, a chair on one side by its head, a bedside cabinet on the other, a wardrobe, a table with another chair, a sink with a towel rail and three hooks behind the door. On the walls were old black and white photos of Forest Gate, blown up and framed. The window looked out to the side wall of the next door house.

Cleo removed the dirty towels from the rail and tossed them by the door. She replaced them with the clean ones she'd brought in. But she wasn't here to change towels. That was her alibi. Might there be something that would tell her more about George, and his relationship with Clyde?

The room was fairly tidy. George hadn't much to make it untidy, just a small suitcase, the contents of which had been placed about the room. Shaving gear and electric toothbrush by the sink. In the bedside cabinet she found socks and underwear. Nothing else. Nor under the mattress or the bed. In the wardrobe a pair of trousers and a shirt were on hangers. Lonely items, with the shelves and floor bare.

Cleo took a chair and placed it by the wardrobe. She stood on it to see the top of the wardrobe. Nothing except bits of fluff. She would dust it when George left. Not leave it for a complaint on TripAdvisor.

Under the wardrobe, deep in the corner, she found it.

Chapter 10

Jack had gone home for lunch. He lived only five minutes' walk up the road, and had thought of inviting Larry back, but decided he needed to be by himself to think things out. And his place was something of a mess.

He could have eaten in Cleo's garden but it was over peopled. He'd be stuck talking to Larry, or to Martin who had come down and was struggling with a tent at the far end of the lawn, a few yards from where they were dumping their soil. Jack had just emptied a wheelbarrow and saw him fighting with poles and the canvas. So he'd helped out, it was a break and he could see immediately the problem. The tent was one of those old fashioned prism-shaped affairs, and Martin was having trouble with the ridge pole. He was trying to put it inside when it had to go outside to hold the flysheet away from the inner tent.

They had a laugh over it. That was the thing about tents, you forgot from one year to the next how you'd put it up last time. Jack left him opening the flaps. Next dump of soil, he saw Martin laid out on the sleeping bag snoozing.

All right for some.

He wondered about his background. His mother Cleo was mixed race, light brown, her son was darker suggesting his dad was black.

So what of that?

Are we all racists? Noting differences in people, instant evaluation, for better and for worse. The scouring of bodies. Colours, shapes, weights, blemishes. Judging, begrudging, putting in categories.

Who wins in this dog show? What is the prize?

Jack and Larry had finished the digging by lunchtime. Jack said they'd have an hour's break. Normally he'd have half an hour but considering doctor's orders he extended it. Larry could do with it too.

At home, Jack made tea. At least that wasn't off limits. He looked at his medication, the bottle and the papers it came with. Metformin, whatever that was. He was supposed to take one with breakfast. Well, he'd missed that, so he'd have it now. He took the tablet with water. It was supposed to lower blood sugar and the dose would be increased week on week, Dr Aziz had explained, until he was taking three a day.

Jack put his lunch on a plate, the one he'd made this morning before his visit to the surgery. He stared at the four slices of white bread made into two large cheese sandwiches. It was high carbs, it was white bread. Two sources of sin. There wasn't much else in the house, nothing healthy anyway.

He ate one sandwich and drank his tea. And was still hungry. Jack cut the remaining sandwich in half and ate it. He felt better, and virtuous. He'd cut back 25% on his normal lunch.

Jack had a second cup of tea. The half sandwich stared at him. Dared him. It was obvious what was going to happen. Why fight it?

He ate the remaining half, and told himself that it wasn't a fry up. And he'd taken his medication. So a modicum of virtue.

Tomorrow. He would start then. Today, it had been dropped on him. Out of the blue. He was unprepared for the new regime. Tomorrow, he would be part of the new world. He'd wake up knowing where he was.

Tomorrow was always a great day to do things. He could see the evasion. Kid's stuff. It had to be today. Or it would always be tomorrow.

Jack took the empty plate into the kitchen so it wouldn't remind him of his weakness. The unwashed dishes in the sink accused him. He managed to force the plate amongst them, and turned to leave, then recalled Mia was coming after school, and forced himself to stand at the sink.

Imagine you are getting paid for this, he told himself.

Jack washed the dishes. It was his penance. Why did he always leave them to pile up? Because it seemed such an endless, repetitive, and pointless task. His mother said he thought too much. Just wash the dishes.

Amidst the suds and warm water, it wasn't so bad. Simple enough. Evasion was a habit. Imagining he was getting paid for it had worked. But it wouldn't work twice, as he wasn't so stupid. Or was he?

Drunks are stupid. Living on junk food is stupid. You know there's a payback. There were a lot of boxes he could tick. Except he wasn't a drunk, not this moment, here and now, and he had no intention of going that way. So delete that box. That left food. It was why he'd come back home. Food, food, it was all about food. It would be the life and death of him.

Chapter 11

Back to work. All the digging had been done before lunch. Jack left Larry levelling the ground with a rake while he made the wooden frame. Its purpose was to hold the wet concrete in while it set.

Jack cut the planks to size, four to go on the sides of the hole they had dug that morning. Together they put them in place. Then using another plank, long enough to cross from side to side, with a spirit level he tested the level. This was crucial, no slope allowed, it had to be dead level. This required a little earth moving here and there. A job not to be rushed, or there would be problems when the concrete was poured.

Happy with the level of the frame, Jack banged in wooden pegs to hold it in place. As he was doing so, Beryl appeared at the French windows.

'You're early,' called Larry, spotting her.

'Can I have a word?' She beckoned her brother over to the patio.

'Something's up,' mumbled Larry as he put down the rake and crossed the lawn. His face was streaked with soil where he'd wiped his hands across.

Beryl sat down at the patio table. She was dressed for the office in her navy blue dress suit and white blouse. Her hair was tied back in an efficient ponytail.

Larry sat down keeping his hands away from the table. 'I don't want to get everything dirty,' he said. 'Should wash.'

'Leave it,' she said. From her stern expression, he could see she wasn't here for small talk.

'Why you early?' he said cautiously.

She flapped a hand dismissively. 'I had to send back to the client an account full of errors. Can't do anything until they've corrected them. At a loose end, I phoned your office.'

That hit him in the stomach. She'd found out. His meddling sister.

'Why?' he said weakly.

'I was thinking of going to the theatre, that Pinter play, thought you might like to come.'

Panic was rising. How much had the office told her?

'The woman I spoke to didn't know who you were,' she said, giving a short, mirthless laugh. 'She asked someone else, and was told that you'd left two months ago.'

He shrugged. That couldn't be argued with. What else had they told her?

'Why the secret?' she said.

She didn't know. He was silent as she watched and waited. At once frightened of her and wanting to hit her. Just like their childhood when he was the reluctant babysitter, knowing if he struck her she'd tell Mum.

At last, looking down at the table, playing with a twig, he said, 'Everyone in the family is so work focussed. Defined by it. Workers and skivers.' He flicked away the twig.

'She said you were fired.'

'I was. Useless at my job. Now you know.' He stood up. 'I should get back to work.'

'Why were you sacked?'

He smiled. 'They didn't call the police, if that's what you want to know.'

'Let's be grateful for small mercies,' she said, adding after a pause, 'It has to be something you are ashamed of. Coming here three days a week, heading off each morning in your suit, with all the appearance of doing a day's work... I assume Jean doesn't know.'

'Are you going to tell her?'

She was tapping the tabletop with her fingers. 'I've never got on with Jean, as you know. She didn't approve of my divorce. She informed me marriage is for life. Through thick and thin, in sickness and in health. Just forget the affair with his secretary, she told me. I should forgive him, be magnanimous.'

'Typical Jean, full of good advice. Asked for or not,' he said. Then added, 'I've emailed her.'

'Told her you are not working?'

'No. That's not her business now. Told her I am not coming back.'

'By email?' She shook her head. 'Oh Larry. Isn't that rather cowardly?'

'Of course,' he said. 'Utterly. But I didn't see anything to be gained by telling her face to face. She'd suggest counselling. Heaven forbid.' He laughed, taking a few seconds to control himself at the image of the pair of them with a counsellor. 'Can you imagine it? She'd do all the talking, I'd do all the seething.'

'What did you say in the email? When did you send it?'

'I sent it lunchtime. I was on my own. Jack had gone home to eat. So I emailed: goodbye and good riddance. Well, not quite so rude. I said that I wasn't coming back. We were finished.' He giggled, barely getting the words out. 'I told her I'd been having an affair for two months.'

'Larry!' She was open mouthed. 'You told her what?'

'I wanted to burn my bridges.'

'I'm sure she'll forgive you.' She smirked, thinking of her sister-in-law's reaction to her own break up. After a few seconds, she added, 'You haven't been having an affair, have you?'

'No such luck.'

He had remained standing, watching Jack who had come in the side gate with a wheelbarrow of hardcore.

Beryl waved at him, Jack nodded, both hands on the wheel-barrow handles. He pushed it across the lawn, brother and sister gazing after him for want of other distraction as he tipped the load into the hole.

'Have we done?' said Larry. 'I really should help out.'

'Is he paying you?'

'No. That wasn't the deal. This is to keep me occupied while I figure out what to do with my life.'

'Well, it got you leaving Jean,' she said. 'Not bad so far.' Then added, 'Pity about the job.'

'Water under the bridge,' he said. 'Manual work is good for me. It helps me think. I'll sort something out.'

'If it's a question of money,' she said, 'I could...'

He held up a hand to halt her. 'Don't start offering, Beryl. It's humiliating. You negotiated a good deal here for me. Thanks for that. But I don't want my little sister propping me up.'

'If you need it, just ask. There's just the two of us now, I feel responsible.'

'Don't.'

'You could try being straight with me.'

'All families lie,' he said. He stood up to leave. 'Or keep secrets.'

'What do you mean?'

'You and Cleo.'

'No comment.'

'I'll take that as a yes.' He bent down and kissed her on the cheek.

'Yuk! You've smudged me with your grime.' She rubbed her cheek. 'Be off with you. More than enough for one afternoon.'

Larry left her and waited for Jack at the hole, levelling a heap of the hardcore with a spade to no great effect. He kept his back turned to his sister, having told her more than enough. The power she had over him. Always had.

Jack came with another barrowful and tipped it into the hole.

He said, 'I've left another shovel out in the drive by the hardcore stack. Take the barrow and refill it. I'll level this. We alternate.'

'Sounds good.'

Larry headed away, glad to be purposeful. His life was slightly less of a lie, but still enough of a tangle for him not to want to admit more to his sister or to Jack. That was the problem with admissions, it was like a sleeve unravelling, you couldn't help pulling at the ragged ends.

They worked on, alternating. One getting a barrow of hardcore, the other levelling. And then a swapover.

Jack wheeled past Beryl at the table. She was smoking a cigarette, half doing a crossword puzzle.

'Got the family working,' she said.

'Want to take over the wheelbarrow?'

'One fifty an hour,' she said.

'I'll accept if it's pennies.'

'More than my brother's getting. But no thank you, Jack.'

He almost said, no one is forcing him, but didn't. He pushed on, wishing she didn't smoke. Smoking always made him think of drinking. Could he go out with a smoker? She was attractive. Yes, he could. Quite severe in her work clothes, though he liked the ponytail, the hair off her face, quite kissable. Pity about the cigarette and her sharpness.

Cleo came through the open French windows. She was in an apron, her hair in a cook's hat.

'Need spinach from the vegetable garden,' she said crossing the patio.

'Might I have a word first,' said Beryl, putting aside the half done crossword and pen.

'Of course.'

Cleo took a chair, taking care to be away from the cigarette smoke, curling in the breeze. Smoking was not allowed in the house. Though, from time to time, guests smoked in their rooms. Filthy habit, she had to turn a blind eye, or go crazy.

But something was up, she knew. Beryl and her formal chats. Never good. Keep calm and wait for it. The cow.

'What can I do for you?' she said.

Beryl inhaled deeply, and then blew out a smoke ring.

She said, 'Larry is having some financial difficulty at the moment. I think he should have free board. Don't you?'

Cleo was thrown back. After all she was already giving, and now more. Would the woman ever stop?

'He's only paying half now,' she exclaimed, keeping her voice down as she was aware of her son in the tent.

'So it should be easier to make it free.' Beryl smiled. 'Halfway there.'

'I can't do it,' exclaimed Cleo, her empty hands emphasising her plea. 'You pay nothing, and you want him free too? How am I to make a living?'

'Come on, Cleo. Be creative. I'm only here three days a week. You have another four days to rake in the cash.'

'I have four rooms. That's all. As it is I hardly have a room myself.'

'Larry goes free. From this week. And he will be staying all week from now on.' She stubbed out her cigarette in the tower ash tray.

Cleo covered her face with her hands, elbows on the table. In her darkness, she said, 'You're a bitch, Beryl.'

'Don't cheat the tax man, Cleo.'

'This isn't possible. Can't be happening. I have built up a business, and you...' She uncovered her face, bit her lip and said, 'I'm going to go to the Inland Revenue. 'Fess up. Do a deal with the man.'

'Got the money?'

'You're an absolute cow. You know I haven't got it. I spent it on the extension to make the fourth bedroom.'

Beryl was lighting another cigarette as she spoke. 'They'll want the money, I can assure you. And if you haven't got it, they'll demand you sell the house. That's if they don't take it from you.'

'You're crushing me, Beryl. If I go under, where will you be?'

'I told you it was stupid building your summerhouse. But would you listen? Of course, you wouldn't.' She drew in smoke. 'I know how money works, dear. Watching you, it's like a gambler throwing his cufflinks into the pot.'

'I have to have that summerhouse,' she exclaimed. 'Have to. It'll be my room. Then there'll be four free rooms in the house. I had to spend the money because of what you're doing to me.'

'Blame me. Go on. You cheat your tax, and blame me. Make me the devil in this, if it suits you.'

Cleo bit her knuckle, breathing heavily, as she watched Beryl smoking, in her office wear and light make-up. The complete business woman. See an angle – home in and grab.

'I'll get the spinach,' she said rising.

Chapter 12

Jack, raking the hardcore, caught a few words between the women. Plainly an argument, and one that Beryl was winning. He strained to hear more, but much was lost, though Cleo's words burst out from time to time. Beryl had some power over Cleo, more than just a guest over a landlady. It was about money. He'd caught that much. Had Cleo borrowed off her? He recalled Larry saying his sister had negotiated a deal with Cleo so he could have 50% off. Did she want even more?

Keep working, don't look their way. Play the innocent.

What mess had Cleo got herself into? This wasn't looking good. Would he get paid? He'd had half payment from Cleo but much of that had gone on materials. Oh, not again. He'd had a number of set-tos with clients over money in the last year. Some over the work, others where the client either didn't have the cash or was trying to pull a fast one. Too often, he'd lost out.

He had to have a chat with her. Though she could easily lie. The deal was half now, half on completion. He could imagine it: the cement dry, the shed assembled, only to be told she'd send the balance next week. And then the next week, always the next week. Until he went through the hassle of small claims court. And won, and still didn't get paid, because she didn't have it.

Beryl had got in first.

What a pessimist he was! Imagining the worst. Maybe he'd heard wrong. And maybe he hadn't.

Larry was crossing the lawn with a wheelbarrow of hardcore. He stopped at the hole edge and tipped the load in.

'My turn,' said Jack.

He took the barrow and headed off. Cleo was in the vegetable garden pulling spinach. She gave him a wave, he gave one back. He'd have a word with her when he'd done this load. He passed the patio. Beryl had gone in. Jack went down the alley to the front of the house.

When he'd returned with a full wheelbarrow, Cleo was sitting at the table with Martin, a bunch of spinach in front of her. They stopped talking as he approached.

'The job's getting on well, I see,' said Cleo.

'We'll lay the concrete tomorrow,' he said, stopping for a moment. 'Might I have a word later, before I go?'

'Of course. Is there a problem?'

He might have voiced his discomfort, but not with her son there.

'A work thing,' he said dismissively. 'Talk to you later.'

He headed to the workings. He had to catch her alone, not that easy in this place.

Cleo and Martin watched Jack head away.

He said, 'You can hear everything in that tent.'

Cleo indicated Jack. 'Sh.' Then back to her son, quietly. 'Everything?'

Martin had showered, hair washed, and he'd shaved. He was wearing a clean pair of jeans and a long sleeved sweatshirt without the grease of his travels.

He said, 'I know she's blackmailing you.'

'She's a one hundred per cent dyed-in-the-wool bitch.'

'And staying here free. Gratis, for nothing. I got that. Her brother is paying half and she wants him to go free too. Is that right?'

'Yes. That's the gist of it.'

'Because you owe a fortune in tax?'

61

She shrugged. He knew it all. Would he use it against her? Surely not. Not even Martin would play that dirty.

'I could give her a scare,' he said.

'What do you mean?'

He pushed his fingers through his bushy hair and smiled. He was so handsome now that he was clean. Face gleaming, he had her bone structure, his father's hair and colouring. She could almost forgive the past transgressions.

'I wait in her room, behind the door. Leap out as she comes in, and put a knife to her throat,' he said, indicating the knife at his own throat with the saw of his hand. 'I tell her, next time I will slice through her windpipe, if she doesn't stop.'

Cleo was aghast. 'She'd leave here and go straight to the Inland Revenue. And probably the cops too.' She held out her hands as if to fend off the helpful hitman, wondering what he'd really been up to in South America. 'Thank you for the offer,' she said, 'but I can do without that sort of help.'

He shrugged. 'Give me a nod, if you change your mind.'

Larry came by them with an empty wheelbarrow. He smiled and headed up the alley.

'This is like being on a traffic island,' said Martin. 'First one, then the other. I'm getting dizzy.' He watched Larry heading away. 'He's the one she wants living here for nothing?'

'The very one. Larry, brother of the bitch accountant.'

Martin picked at his clean nails. 'He's in trouble, you know. Not working. Pretending. Fired two months ago.'

'Oh!' exclaimed Cleo, glancing about her as she had raised her voice, but Jack was raking and not looking their way. 'I did wonder about Larry. Not working. Well, well. That accounts for his sister's hit on me.'

'I'm just lying back, on my sleeping bag, in the tent. Minding my own business. And everyone is spilling the beans like I'm not in there.' He laughs. 'The walls are just thin canvas and everyone's treating them like they are three thickness of brick.' He tapped the table with his fingernails. 'I've got another angle,' he said smiling, obviously pleased he could help his mother.

'No knives, please.'

'No. This is about Larry. As I said, he's not working. Got fired from his job two months ago. And he won't say why.'

'Ah, that's interesting. There might be something there.'

'I've been fired a few times,' said Martin. 'For not working, nicking stuff, shagging the boss's daughter in the stockroom...'

'Spare me the details,' she said putting up her hands as a barrier to further information. 'I know you were never good at holding down jobs.'

'Forget me. I'm thinking about Larry. Why they fired him.'

'I can't imagine sexual harassment...' she said, 'but you never know...'

'Dealing drugs?'

'Nor that. He's too straight.'

'Fraud?'

'Surely they'd have the cops on him. Unless it was just small beer.'

'Porn.' He clapped his hands. 'I bet you!'

'Sh!' she said, looking at Jack working.

'There's no one in the tent,' he said with a chuckle.

She smiled and tapped him on the nose with a finger. 'What makes you think it's porn?'

'He emailed his wife, telling her he's not coming back. So getting no nookie there. For quite some time, I reckon.'

'Could be call girls?' she surmised. 'Middle aged, on the shy side. How do we find out?'

'I could go in his room and take a look at his laptop.'

'More likely on his phone,' she said.

She was pleased they were doing something together, even if it was somewhat dubious. So much better than her shouting at him.

'I'm sure I could get hold of that,' he said.

'Make it temporary,' she said. 'Just a look. No thievery.'

Chapter 13

Jack and Larry worked on through the afternoon, alternating, one at the hole levelling, the other filling the wheelbarrow and bringing it out, switching over once the load was emptied. It was an OK way to work, sharing the effort. Jack had a second wheelbarrow in his lock-up but he'd been expressly told by the doctor not to overexert himself.

Beryl came out with a tray of tea. He and Larry joined her on the patio. There were three custard tarts. Jack shouldn't have taken one, but he did. And said to himself, tomorrow.

They talked about the weather, and the state of the sky for his telescope tonight. The sky was three quarters clear, a little breeze. He told them to wrap up warm.

'Cleo does a good barbecue,' said Beryl. 'That'll keep us warm.'

They kept off the personal. Jack knew more than Beryl realised. One of those situations where if the three had pooled their knowledge, all would have been wiser. But Jack didn't know Beryl, much as he'd like to, and she didn't know him. Maybe tonight, but then he'd have Mia with him. And the telescope.

His time would be rationed.

Larry and Jack went back to work. They had switched to sand, a last covering before the concrete. In an hour, it was all done and levelled. Jack looked it over. Looking good. A decent size for a shed. OK, summerhouse. He'd seen the plan. A large room, a verandah even. She must have the money to pay him. Surely?

He went out to his van and brought in the compactor. A machine, about the size of a lawn mower, powered by a long lead that went into the house via the French windows and plugged into an electric socket. The compactor had a flat plate bottom which trembled up and down when switched on, compacting the surface. Without it, the hard-core below the sand would settle unevenly over time, causing the concrete above to sink and crack.

Jack let Larry do the compacting. The machine was a novelty for him, his face beaming as he went up and down the area, as if it were a new Christmas toy. Jack tidied away as there was no more that could be done that day.

A little past four o'clock, they finished work. The aim tomorrow was to lay the concrete. More sand would be needed on top, as the compacting had dropped the surface a couple of inches. Half an hour or so to correct that, then bring in the cement mixer.

Larry shook Jack's hand. 'I've enjoyed today. It's been good for me. Much better than going round another museum, or doing the crossword in Starbucks. Do you want a hand tomorrow?'

'You've been OK. Better than I thought you'd be,' admitted Jack. 'No arguments. Done what you're told.'

'So it's on?'

'I can't pay you, Larry. This job's too tight.'

'I'm not expecting pay. Call it work experience.' He laughed. 'At my age! Ring in the changes. Another mid life crisis. I've got all the negatives. Fired from my job, ended my marriage. I didn't tell you that. Well, I've told you now. Is that positive or negative? Time will tell. I emailed my wife, said goodbye, dear, I've been having an affair the last couple of months.' He laughed uncontrollably, tears welling, struggling to get the words out in his mirth. 'I wonder how that hit her. Oh dear. I'd love to have been a fly on the wall. Seen her face. I bet she was at work. Read it twice, three times, slammed her laptop shut.'

Jack could imagine it. The office, the email, Larry's wife weeping in a toilet stall.

'Rather brutal,' he said.

Larry wiped his eyes with the back of his hand. 'There was no other way. I had to tell her from a distance.'

'And the affair?'

'A bit of nonsense, but she wouldn't know. To make it clear I am not changing my mind. Finito. Done with. I am a free man. I can make my own choices.'

He shook a fist at a cloud as if his wife might be up there, glaring down at him. He turned to Jack, back on earth.

'I have to get a job. A proper job. Heaven knows what.'

Chapter 14

Jack left his van outside Cleo's when he went home after work, but took the wheelbarrow. His telescope was on the heavy side, so he'd use the wheelbarrow to ferry it with the mount to tonight's do.

A little way from Cleo's, Jack halted. He remembered that he'd meant to have a word with her about money. Though what exactly was he going to say? *I'm worried you haven't got the money to pay me*. But really, what was she likely to say to that? If she didn't have the money, she'd lie. Or she might take umbrage that he'd dare to suggest it. No way to deal with a client.

All he could do was cross his fingers. Asking her about her financial situation would be pointless, no matter what he sensed. He pushed on with the wheelbarrow. You work on trust. Sometimes you get screwed, and even if you can see it coming, what can you do?

He looked up at the sky as he pushed along, the wheel rumbling. Maybe three quarters clear. If it stayed that way, it'd be an OK night for the telescope. But you never knew, cloud could come in quickly and cover the sky. Jack had had frustrating weeks with cloudy skies, not once getting out with the telescope. He wondered if it clouded over, could he still go to the barbecue?

Worry about that later. Except it was dinner for him and Mia. Take the scope then, and if it was cloudy, say it might clear. Which was no lie.

Outside his house, Jack left the wheelbarrow in the front yard. No one would take it from there, an old stained builder's barrow. Then he reflected, they just might, and that would mean hassles at the job tomorrow as it was needed. The alternative was to leave it in the outer hallway, just past the front door. But it was only a short hallway; the wheelbarrow would make it difficult opening the front door.

The doors of the two flats faced the front door, his for the upstairs and the other for the old lady downstairs. They didn't get on. She'd complained about his music and the sound of his television. And a couple of times, she'd banged on her ceiling with a walking stick to protest about the noise of his lovemaking.

Jack tried to avoid her. If he said any more than good morning, she'd be off on a diatribe about something he'd done or was likely to do. Would he risk a row with the wheelbarrow? Oh, it was just this once. Give and take, he couldn't let her dictate to him. He had a right to live here as much as she did.

He pushed the wheelbarrow in through the front door, over the threshold. It went from front to back, the front almost touching his flat door, the handles only a few inches from the front door. Not on. This was a communal area; he had to accept it. She wouldn't be able to get out of the house. The thought pleased him for an instant, but it'd be hassles for ever more.

Jack took the wheelbarrow back out and left it on the path by the bins.

See how considerate he was.

He went in and opened his flat door. When he got upstairs, there was Mia in the sitting room. She'd thrown her full backpack and outdoor jacket on to the sofa, and was at the table on her laptop. He immediately recognised the page she was on, one for type 2 diabetes.

'Why you looking at that?' he said.

'This.' She held up the bottle of medication that he'd left on the table at lunchtime. Somewhat careless of him. 'Metformin. I looked it up. And it says it's prescribed for polycystic ovary syndrome and for type 2 diabetes. You haven't got ovaries.' She grinned. 'So it has to be diabetes.'

'Smart girl.'

'Mum always says with all your junk food you'd get diabetes.'

'Smart mother.' He almost added daft dad, but was feeling niggled at being got at as soon as he'd entered the flat.

'You could go blind,' said Mia reading from her screen, 'lose toes, or a limb, not be able to work. And as for your sex life...'

'Enough,' he interrupted. 'It's early stage. And even reversible if I do the right things.'

She turned to him. 'Will you?'

Mia was in her school uniform, a light blue shirt and navy trousers. Her hair was in a ponytail, the same chestnut brown as her mother's. Mother and daughter were the same height, figures not unalike. Mia had filled out this year, going from girl to woman.

'Will I what?' he said.

She sighed heavily. 'Eat properly, Dad. Give up junk food. Your blood sugar is too high. If it stays that way, you'll be on insulin until you go into a coma and die.'

'Do you talk that way to all your patients, Doctor Bell?'

'I like to give them the hard truth.'

He laughed. Quite what he was laughing at he wasn't sure.

'Well you may laugh,' she said. 'I looked in the cupboard and the fridge. And there wasn't much. But I threw out the white bread and jam.'

He was aghast, his daughter dictating his diet.

'How dare you!' he exclaimed. 'You don't throw my food out.'

She ducked as if he'd hit her.

'I only threw out the heavy carbs. I don't know how you can eat white bread... Yuk.' She grimaced in distaste.

'It makes the best toast,' he said.

'And jam?'

'It's good on toast.'

'Have you heard of five a day?'

'Stop it,' he exclaimed. 'Right now. I've had all this from the doctor. I shall improve my diet. But you have no right to chuck my food out. What am I going to have for break-fast and lunch tomorrow?'

'We could go shopping.'

'Have you got any homework?'

'Don't change the subject,' she said. 'We need proper food. Low carbs, fruit and veg. Wholemeal bread, no pota-toes. It's dead easy. Anyway, I'm hungry.'

'You could've had some bread and jam,' he said. 'But you threw it out. Do you pay for it? Of course not.'

'I could stay at Mum's. And leave you to die.'

'I can't take this any more!' He stormed into the kitchen.

'And I washed the stove top!' she yelled.

He closed the kitchen door behind him. Yes, she'd cleaned the stove. It had been pretty mucky with fry up splatter. He looked in the rubbish bin. There was half a loaf of bread with a splurge of red jam on top. What had she done with the jar? He spotted it on the draining board, washed, pristine clean for recycling.

Maybe he should be recycled himself. Thrown out and melted down. He sank into a chair, angry and weary. The cheek of Mia. How could she? She had come in from school and, once she'd sussed he had diabetes, she'd coolly thrown out half a loaf of bread, and a jar of jam. That was like throwing three quid away. Is this teenage rebellion, saving the planet by throwing out white bread?

It was on the cards that Cleo wouldn't pay him. And his daughter was binning hard earned cash.

Jack stayed in the kitchen, too angry and depressed to go back into the sitting room. He would only blast at her. That's what you did with kids, the world's having a go at you, you move down the food chain to assuage your anger.

It was Cleo, the risk of non payment, it was diabetes. He hadn't been much affected at the doctor's. But it had been sinking in all day. He'd have to change and he wasn't much good at change. And there was his daughter making it seem like putting on clean clothes. Or he'd die, as she'd just told him. She had more sense than he had sometimes.

Not all the time.

There had been boyfriend trouble over Christmas. She'd been seeing an 18 year old. Alison, out shopping, had caught her arm in arm with him, fully made up in short skirt and high-heeled shoes. That had been the mother of all rows. The skirt and shoes belonged to Alison. The relationship had petered out in a few weeks. Alison had laid down the law, he had supported her. Was this Mia getting her own back?

He must tell her the rules in this flat. He was the adult. He must keep his temper, but throwing out good food wasn't on. Not good food, he conceded. But if she wasn't here, he'd have made himself some toast and jam. Enough to stave off hunger, until the barbecue tonight. What other food was there? There must be something, a bite somewhere.

He stood up and instantly felt dizzy, rocking on his feet and holding on to the table. Then sank slowly back into the chair and closed his eyes, the darkness spinning in his head. He felt shivery, legs hollow.

Doctor Aziz had explained the dizziness to him. His blood either had too much sugar in it or too little. And when it had too little, he was like a plane out of fuel, liable to go into a dive. So get some fuel. Anything would do. He looked in the fridge. Bacon, cheese, margarine and milk. He took out the milk and poured himself a glassful. And then went to the cupboard. There was a bag of sugar. Mia was in the other room, so no teenage lecture. Jack put four teaspoons into the milk and stirred it away. Emergency calories. He sank back the milk, drinking it all.

He sat back down. Very aware of the weakness of his body. But the sugared drink worked. And in a couple of minutes, he felt better. Let's make it up with Mia. He went out into the sitting room. She wasn't there. Neither was her school-bag. Oh heavens, had she run off to her mum's? He checked the bedroom, just in case, not there, the bathroom empty.

This was all he needed. Things piling up. He sat at the table and dialled her number. It rang and rang, and went to voicemail. He tried to think what to say and closed the call as he wasn't sure what words in what order.

She most likely had gone to Alison's. Alison though had school business and wouldn't be back till late. How about the library, to do some homework. Or to the park, to a friend. He'd bet Alison's. Jack dialled again, and went once more to voicemail. She was purposely not picking up.

He said, 'Come home, Mia. I'm not angry now. It was only bread and jam. Junk, I agree.'

Jack wanted to say more but words stalled. Should he call Alison, tell her their daughter had stormed off in a huff? Alison would ask him why, he'd have to come up with some banal reason. But wasn't she in a meeting, or something like?

At least, he could look down the road. She hadn't been gone long. He rose. Not giddy, so the sugar had done its work, but it wouldn't last long. One thing at a time. His daughter. He went down the stairs and opened the flat door. In the small hallway was Mrs Brown, the old lady from downstairs, with her basket on wheels.

She said, 'Is that your wheelbarrow by the dustbins?'

'It is,' he said.

'I hope it's not going to stay there.'

He had to stifle a comeback. He didn't know how old she was. Late 70s, early 80s, of that order. Pretty healthy with it. Might hang on for another twenty years. More's the pity. She wore a long check green coat and what Alison would call 'sensible', black shoes. Her hair was dyed brown, very neat, her face wrinkled, lightly made up with purple lipstick.

'I'm going to move it shortly,' he said. 'Have you seen my daughter?'

'Yes,' said Mrs Brown. 'I saw her walking down the road towards the high street. I asked her about the wheelbarrow. She said she knew nothing about it. And told me to ask you.'

'And you have,' he said.

'It's so unsightly,' she said, 'a dirty wheelbarrow.'

She turned the key in her lock, and opened the door, evidently having said her piece and expecting to be obeyed. She went inside, pulling the wheeled basket behind, and closing the door on him.

They had never had a friendly conversation. She was always demanding that he do something. Turn the noise down, clear up the mess on the path, put down thick carpet and foam rubber under his bed. Mia had ceased practising her saxophone at Jack's after two of Mrs Brown's complaints.

At least he hadn't got into a row this time. He went outside, closing the front door quietly. Not risking another downstairs complaint, how he or Mia always slammed the door. Seeing the wheelbarrow, he had to admit it was somewhat in the way, unsightly you might say. But what could he do with it? He should have brought the van back, even though it was just a hundred yards or so, and carried the telescope in that.

Why not do it now? One less quarrel.

And he thought, take the wheelbarrow with. Please somebody, though he doubted Mrs Brown could ever be pleased. Jack set off down the road with the wheelbarrow. He couldn't see Mia, though he peered far along the street, through the tree-lined pavement. Buds were thickening on the branches, a few had broken into leaf. On a rooftop a bird was singing its heart out. Surprising how much sound a small body could make. Mrs Brown would have a few words to say, especially all that early morning racket.

Arriving at his van, outside Cleo's house, he encountered George. He was wearing a green baseball cap.

'Did you get to the British Museum?' said Jack. Not really caring if he had or hadn't, but words were needed.

'Every single floor.' He blew out his cheeks. 'What a lot of it! All the booty of Empire.'

'Did you see Clyde there?'

'Not unless he was hiding under a mummy.' He stopped and waved a finger. 'You said you knew him from Cumberland School. I reckoned I did too. He wasn't called Clyde though. Paul something or other.'

'Blake,' exclaimed Jack. The surname had come to him. 'Might not be him. It was 20 years ago...'

'You could be right. Just looks so like him. Remembered me yet?'

'I think so,' he said, though he hadn't. George plainly wanted to be remembered.

'Time passes,' he said, looking at his watch. 'Must have a shower and make some calls before the barbecue tonight. I'm looking forward to seeing your telescope.'

'The sky's pretty clear,' said Jack. There were only a few clouds amongst the blue. But he was wondering whether he would come at all, with Mia missing. He couldn't possibly go out if she was not back.

'See you later then,' said George and went down the path to the door.

Jack considered what to do with the wheelbarrow. He could lock it in the van, but why not leave it on the drive. There was no car there. He wheeled it in behind the cubical bag of sand. He lifted a sack of cement and put it inside the wheelbarrow to discourage anyone from taking it. And then another on top.

As he dropped the sack, a wave of weakness hit him.

Not too bright, heavy lifting in his state. Jack supported himself on the garden wall and breathed deeply. Not too bad, just a temporary thing, but must mean low blood sugar. He must eat something. There was only bacon and cheese at home. He was out; he could shop.

Where was Mia? Worrying about himself should be more than enough. He dialled. Pick up, pick up! There was the pause before the connection...

A phone was ringing in the street.

Jack strode out onto the pavement. There was Mia coming towards him, maybe ten yards off.

'Hello,' he said, as she came up. 'I came to look for you. Where have you been?'

'I was going to the library to do some homework,' she said. 'Instead, I went shopping. I shouldn't have thrown your bread away.'

'Forget it. What have you got for us?'

She held out a Co-op shopping bag, and opened it by the handles to let him see the contents.

'Wholemeal bread,' she said, pulling out a brown, sliced loaf like a magician drawing a rabbit from a hat. She handed it to him.

'Good one.' Though he wasn't fond of wholemeal.

'Peanut butter, muesli, bananas.' More and more rabbits she handed to her father. 'Greek yoghurt and oranges.'

'All the right stuff,' he said, his arms overwhelmed in healthy goodness. 'Beats jam and white bread, I admit. Let's go home and eat. I'm famished.'

Chapter 15

They drove the few hundred yards home. Jack told Mia about the barbecue and telescope do later on.

'What the people like?' she said tentatively.

'They're OK,' he said, 'a mixture.' Hoping she could cope. Though there would be the crutch of the telescope to support her. She knew her astronomy after years of going on the Flats with him.

At home, they had a light meal with the food that Mia had bought: a bowl of muesli with Greek yoghurt, a peanut butter sandwich and a banana.

'Wasn't so bad, was it?' said Mia. It could have been Alison talking.

'That's the healthiest tea I've had in ages,' he said, still a little hungry. 'I was aching to put some sugar in the yoghurt. A bit sharp for my taste.'

'You'll get used to it.'

Jack wondered whether he ever would. Or would he always yearn for sugar? But he'd eaten, that was the main thing. Regular meals, Doctor Aziz had said. His body had warned him of the danger of skipping them with the dizzy spell earlier. He didn't tell Mia of it. It was his problem.

He offered her the money for the food, but she wouldn't take it. There was no point forcing it on her; she was as stubborn as he was. Which he half admired. He'd buy her something, when and if, Cleo paid him.

Jack had a shower. As he soaped himself, he was feeling fine, utterly healthy again. How his body could oscillate, from his current bounce to utter exhaustion. He must take control. Was he going to become one of those food bores: counting the calories, looking at saturated and unsaturated fats, how many grams of sugar per hundred grams of whatever.

Probably. He was an obsessive.

Mia changed out of her school uniform and then did some homework. Jack went through his astronomy magazine to see what was observable. The centre pages had a map of the night sky with suggestions for telescope observation this month. At quarter past seven, they loaded the telescope and its mount in the van, wrapping them both in a blanket to protect them from the materials and tools in the back of the van.

The sky was darkening as they left, driving the short distance to Cleo's. There, Jack retrieved the wheelbarrow from the drive, having to take out the hefty sacks he'd put in it. Somewhat pointless putting them in at all. Though maybe not, he reflected, the barrow was still there.

You can't prove a negative.

They put the telescope and mount into the wheelbarrow, still in their blanket cocoons. And Jack pushed the barrow down the alley with Mia following. They were both dressed in their telescope garb: warm jackets and scarves, woolly hats, with fingerless gloves in their pockets.

The smell of cooking meat greeted them as they approached the patio. They came out to a halo of light. The guests were seated about the patio, plates on their knees. Jack left the wheelbarrow, at the side, out of the way. It needed to be a bit darker before they set up the scope with the house and patio lights off.

Cleo crossed from the barbecue; she was in a bright floral apron and cook's hat, her brown face shiny with steam and sweat.

'This is my daughter, Mia,' said Jack. 'She knows more astronomy than I do.'

'I don't,' said Mia peeved.

'I'm Cleo. I won't shake your hand, Mia, my hands are greasy. Do help yourselves. There's sausages and chops, salad, and French bread. All on the table.'

She left them and went back to the barbecue.

'I'm going to eat,' said Mia. 'You'd better too.'

She went to the central table where the food was placed on platters. Mia took a plate and began filling it.

Jack hesitated, a little way back from the table. Food was an obstacle course. Mia was not holding back and filling her plate rapidly. He looked around at the others. Larry who had on a cream trilby was sitting by his sister Beryl. She waved at Jack with a fork. He smiled back at her, spidering his fingers in greeting. She'd really gone to town, in a long yellow dress, purple cardigan, and matching yellow, peasant-type scarf tied round her head. He hoped he'd be able to get some time with her, but what with everyone else, not least of all, Mia, and the necessity to be at the telescope, would that happen?

Sitting outside his tent on the lawn was Martin. He had a heaped plate of food and a bottle of beer. He obviously felt an outsider, relegated to the lawn, so was sticking to his territory which didn't include the patio, though obviously allowed a path to the table and back. George was with Cleo at the barbecue in an apron and chef's hat, turning sausages with a slice. Jack knew Cleo could manage perfectly well on her own, but George was one of those men who liked to hold the centre stage at barbecues, reminding Jack of a black celebrity chef on TV.

Clyde was alone, seated near the French windows as if he wanted to slip away. He was Paul Blake from school, Jack was sure of it. He'd changed his name for some reason and didn't want it known. So why come back?

The smell of smoke, mingled with onions and sizzling meat had Jack's stomach gurgling. This was good food. But faced with a cornucopia, what was permissible? He picked up a plate.

'Everything but the French bread,' said Mia. 'Make sure you get some salad.'

'Got it,' he said, accepting the rules, and tentatively took some pasta salad, and then a little lettuce and tomato salad, spreading it out to make it look more than it was. Who was he kidding? A chop and two sausages completed his plate. He looked longingly at the French bread. He always had bread with a meal, now he came to think of it, every meal.

He sat next to Mia. She hadn't spoken to anyone, not surprising as they were all strangers to her. She'd be more part of things when they had the telescope set up.

'I'm making the base for a summer house, over there.' He pointed it out with a fork.

'Working close to home,' she said, half listening as she looked about her. 'A lot of artificial light here,' she said, indicating the patio beam and the spill from the lounge. 'Not good for viewing.'

'Let's get the scope up,' he said. 'Then sort the light out.'

'No point otherwise,' she said.

Beryl came over. Her perfume, reminiscent of lilacs, with the yellow of her gypsy scarf made him spin. It was as well he was with Mia. Some protection from his hormones.

Did she have a boyfriend? Lover?

'Beryl, this is my daughter, Mia,' he said croakily. 'She's the astronomy expert in the family.'

'I'm not,' said Mia with a sigh. 'He always says that. I know a little about astronomy. That's all.'

'That counts as an expert in my company, Mia,' said Beryl. 'I know the moon, and that those twinkly things are stars. I wouldn't know a planet if you hit me with it.'

Mia rolled her eyes, not impressed with this woman's pride in her ignorance.

'A planet is a large body that revolves round a sun,' she said. 'There are eight in our solar system.'

'My very educated mother just served us nine pizzas,' said Beryl rapidly.

'What?' exclaimed Mia.

Beryl ticked off on her fingers: 'Mercury, Venus, Earth, Mars, Jupiter, Saturn, Uranus, Neptune and Pluto. Although your father told me earlier that Pluto has been demoted to a minor planet. Which means it's still a planet, just not in the first division.'

'That's right,' said Mia. 'You're not so dumb at all.'

'Mia!' exclaimed Jack. 'Don't be rude.'

'Let's say forthright,' said Beryl placatingly. 'I might yet win your approval, Mia. There are two pointers in the Plough which point to the Pole Star.'

'True,' nodded Mia.

'And Orion has a belt. And if he didn't, his trousers would fall down.'

Mia giggled.

'Will you show me the telescope later?' said Beryl.

'Yes,' said Mia. 'But you mustn't play stupid.'

'You're quite right to admonish me. Women mustn't apologise for knowing a bit of science. And now I'll leave you and your dad to eat.'

She blew a kiss and left them, returning to Larry.

'Do you fancy her?' said Mia quietly as she walked off.

'Have I your permission?'

'I'm not sure yet.'

He smiled. Her opinion was at least on the positive side of absolute zero.

'She'll improve,' he said. 'Once you show her the stars.'

'So you do fancy her.'

'Ah, but does she fancy me?'

'Course she does.'

Jack considered whether his daughter was being astute or just guessing.

George came over carrying a large platter at shoulder height. He was playing head chef in his apron and white hat, bowing as he offered the steaming burgers, as if this was his restaurant.

'Monsieur et Mademoiselle. 'Avez un ou deux 'amburgers, s'il vous plais. Tous Cordon Bleu. That's the limit of my French, Jack. Courtesy of Cumberland School.'

'Did Bozzo take you for French?'

'Yeh. Dead useless was old Bozzo. Couldn't run a pasty stall at Glastonbury. I'm looking forward to seeing your Newtonian Refractor,' he said. 'See? I remembered.'

'Ten out of ten,' said Jack, taking a burger.

George moved on with his platter, crossing the patio and offering it to Beryl and Larry. Jack watched him walk away. He had made up the name Bozzo, off the cuff, but George said he knew him. And then had quickly changed the subject.

He hadn't been at Cumberland. Why pretend? Presumably to discomfort Clyde, who was there. Clyde who was Paul Blake. And George was fishing, for his own reasons.

Jack cut a piece of burger and examined it on the fork. Was it good or bad in dietary terms? Probably not the best of meat, but it had been fried in its own fat. He stopped himself. He couldn't go on like this, turning over every morsel. Not tonight at least. Just no bread, that would do for starters.

Besides, he'd eaten the salad, and had a bowl of muesli earlier. That must knock up some brownie points. His pancreas must be reconsidering its attitude to insulin.

Sublime optimism, he knew.

Behind the barbecue, Cleo was taking off her apron and cook's hat. Evidently, enough meat had been cooked to satisfy her guests. She came out from behind the grill, flashing her hands.

'Greasy, greasy. Must wash, then I can eat,' she declared as she rushed into the house via the French windows.

It was getting darker, but no stars were visible due to the lights from the lounge and patio. What best to do, thought Jack. If the sitting room was dimmed, curtains closed, the patio light off, that might work. To some extent. Pity there wasn't a moon. You could always see something on the moon, even if the stars were washed out by it.

They finished eating.

'Let's set up,' said Jack.

Jack pushed the wheelbarrow on to the lawn, Mia followed. He wheeled it close to the site where he'd been working that day. There weren't any other options for the set up. The opposite corner of the lawn was ruled out as Martin's tent was there along with the heap of soil and leftover hardcore which was going to be Cleo's rock garden.

Mia unwrapped the mount from its blanket. She opened the three legs and checked for level with the small spirit level on the stage between them. Mia moved the mount a few times, seeking flat ground, as the telescope mustn't be wobbly. Once satisfied, she gave way to Jack who placed the telescope body on the mount and did up the wing nuts.

Cleo came back out into the garden. She had put on make-up and was wearing a thick blue sweater. She approached Clyde who was sitting on his own.

'How's the food?' she asked.

'Fine, fine,' he said. 'No complaints. But I must watch my weight.'

'Mustn't we all,' she said. 'Do you know this area? Jack, the builder, thought he recognised you.'

'I'm not from round here,' he said stiffly. 'I found you on TripAdvisor. Cheap. Good reports. Near the station.'

'You flew in,' she said, trying to bring him out. 'Where from?'

'America,' he said.

'I've a cousin in California,' she said. 'Los Angeles.' She didn't actually know where her cousin was but she was the host, and Clyde was so on his own. 'Whereabouts are you?'

'Canada.'

She was about to say Canada isn't America. But of course it is, it's just that when one says America one usually means the US. Clearly he didn't want to say. Clyde was odd. Nervous and standoffish.

He said, 'I shall be leaving in the morning. After breakfast.'

'I thought you were staying three days.'

'I've changed my mind.'

She wondered whether it had anything to do with Jack recognising him.

'I can't give you a refund.'

'I understand,' he said. 'My plans have changed.'

'Are you interested in astronomy?' she said pointing out where Mia and Jack were setting up.

'No.'

This was a chore; one word answers and no information volunteered. But he was leaving and refused to allow her to cheer him up. She could do no more.

Cleo bent to pick up a plate and noted the bottle of spirits beneath Clyde's seat. He'd said he wasn't going to drink tonight. So much for that. Drunks were a hassle. As she straightened, she smelt his breath; Clyde had had a fair bit already. But at least, she had moved him to her room tonight, should Clyde snore like a bull elephant. She would be sleeping in what had been Clyde's room, next door to him, and hoping earplugs would be sufficient. She would like to buy some noise cancelling earphones, but they were so expensive and she had too many demands on her depleted cash. She had Jack to pay somehow. That did not bear thinking about. And Beryl and her blackmail. There was no other word for it.

The front doorbell rang.

'Someone at the door,' exclaimed Cleo, pleased for an excuse to leave taciturn Clyde.

She hot footed into the lounge to find out who was calling.

Chapter 16

Jack came on to the centre of the patio. He addressed them all. 'Hello, everyone. The telescope is set up. I'm going to turn some lights down or it won't work. Not forever. Promise.'

'We won't know who we're kissing,' called George.

'You should be so lucky,' responded Jack.

He went into the lounge. Way too much light spilling from here. He turned off the centre light and all the side lights but one. He had to leave that as this was the way through to the bathroom. Jack drew the curtains across the French windows.

Where was the patio light switch?

He knew where he'd put it. And there it was, by the side of the window. He turned the light off. And stepped through the curtain on to the patio. A little light came through the curtains, enough to make out shapes, and, as he was adjusting to the darkness, Beryl, standing a few feet away. Her perfume confirmed it.

Jack looked across to the telescope. He could make out the silhouette of Mia and who was that? The trilby had to be Larry. And was that Martin too? She'd be fine for a minute or two.

'I wondered whether I was going to get you alone,' said Beryl.

'Not since we were building pyramids,' he said.

'3, 4, 5. Once I caught a fish alive.'

In a rapid movement, she kissed him on the mouth, holding his cheeks in the flat of her hands. Giving in to flesh and perfume, he clutched her, his hands on the low of her back. Even in the semi darkness, giving in, he knew it was too public.

He broke away. 'Not here,' he whispered.

She stepped to him, pressing her hip against his.

'Where?' she said quietly. She patted his lips with a finger. 'When?'

'Tomorrow,' he said, the soonest he could manage. 'We could go for a meal.' Even as he said it, he was thinking of the problem of food.

'I was thinking of your place,' she said.

'At seven,' he said. 'It's just up the road.'

Cleo came through the curtains with a woman, medium height, on the plump side in a long black coat. Jack separated from Beryl. A respectable distance.

'Where's Larry?' said Cleo, peering about. 'I can hardly see out here.'

'He's at the telescope,' said Jack pointing.

'Jean,' exclaimed Beryl. 'What are you doing here?'

'I'm here to see my husband,' said the woman. 'To find out what's got into him.'

'You've come all the way from Sheffield?'

'I most certainly have. Drastic statements require drastic measures. Where is he?'

'I'll take you to him,' said Cleo.

'I don't think he wants to see you,' said Beryl.

'I'd be obliged if you stay out of my affairs, Beryl. Thank you very much.' She turned to Cleo. 'Take me to my husband, Mrs Dickens.'

Very formal, thought Jack as Cleo led Jean off. Beryl came hurrying after. He was left on the patio as the three women went on to the lawn.

'Cut short your tete a tete,' said George, with a snigger. He was sitting on a chair, barely visible in the poor light with his dark complexion, dark sweater and jeans.

'Just as well,' said Jack.

'I thought she was going to eat you.'

'Quite a meal,' mused Jack, reflecting on the kiss and the cosiness of her body. She was coming to his place tomorrow. Heaven knows what they'd eat. But the way she'd come on to him, it didn't seem eating was high on her agenda. Though he hadn't given her the address. Plenty of time to sort that out tomorrow.

Mia was right. She did fancy him.

And he'd better check on his daughter. There was a group round the telescope, dark shadows against the trees and purple sky. He'd better get there, see what was going on.

'Jean!' exclaimed Larry as he looked up from the telescope eyepiece. 'What are you doing here?'

He was with Mia and Martin when the three women arrived.

'I've come to see you,' she said.

'Well, I don't want to see you,' said Larry. 'I thought I'd made that clear.'

'Thirty-one years of marriage and he doesn't want to see me! An email dismissal. Is that how it's done, Larry?'

'I don't want to talk to you,' he said.

The others had drawn back, almost a ring around the sparring husband and wife.

'Is she here?' said Jean. 'Your mistress.'

'I don't want to talk to you.' He turned to Cleo. 'Please ask her to leave. I don't want her here. I'm a guest. She's not.'

'I am a guest, Larry.' Jean smiled. 'I have booked a room. You cannot avoid me.'

Jack arrived, catching the last comment.

'I have nothing to say to you, Jean. Don't you understand English? Sometimes I wonder.'

'I think you should leave him be, Jean,' said Beryl, standing by her brother. 'He has made himself perfectly clear.'

'You always were an interfering bitch,' exclaimed Jean. 'From the first moment I laid eyes on you.'

'My brother doesn't want you here,' said Beryl. 'He has made that totally plain.'

'Stay out of this please, Beryl,' said Larry quietly.

'I'm just trying to help.'

'Don't.'

Jean smirked at Larry's put-down of his sister.

'Can we talk, dear?' she said, mock affectionately. 'Alone, without an audience.'

'No,' exclaimed Larry.

He stormed off, across the lawn. Jean and Beryl set off after him.

'What a palaver!' said Cleo, her hands going to her head as she watched them heading away. 'Never a dull moment in this place. I opened the door to her, she told me she wanted a single room. So I booked her into the room I was going to sleep in tonight...'

'Where will you sleep?' said Jack.

'In the lounge. On the sofa. I've done it often enough.'

The two of them had separated from Mia and Martin who had gone back to the telescope. Jack came in a little closer.

'Are you all right for money, Cleo?' said Jack quietly.

'Of course I am,' she said. 'What makes you say that?'

'Just something Larry mentioned.'

'Oh that family! The bane of my life. Beryl bullies me, wants this, wants that. Nothing's enough for her. And she protects her brother.'

'Got him half rate,' said Jack.

'He told you that? Well, she did. She is an ace conniver. I'll tell you no more, but if she gets a knife in her back, there'll be no shortage of suspects.'

Mia had her eye to the eyepiece of the telescope. She was explaining to Martin what she was seeing.

'Just getting in tight on Mizar...' she said, turning the focus. 'Almost there.'

'Do you want some snow?' whispered Martin.

'Snow?'

'A snifter. Coke.'

'My dad's here,' she said. 'Just there.' She indicated him a few yards off.

'A pity that. I was thinking we could go upstairs. Have a snort. You know? And see how it goes.'

'I can't. My dad's here.'

'Tomorrow then. We'll sort something out. Have a bit of fun. Give me your phone number.'

'When my dad's gone from here. Now look like you're interested in astronomy...' She spoke up, primarily so her father would hear. 'That's Mizar in the handle of the Plough, also known as the Big Dipper. It looks like one star but in proper darkness, not like this, you can see it's a double star if you have good eyesight. But through the telescope, you can see it is in fact three stars.'

'How come you know so much?' said Martin.

'I've been going out with my dad and the telescope for years. He has his astronomy mags lying around; I read them.' She shrugged. 'I've picked up things. I'd like to go somewhere where the sky is really dark, not like here, but say Dartmoor, with no light pollution.'

'I wish him and my mum would go off and leave us,' whispered Martin. 'I'm sure we'd get on like turtle doves in a birdbath.'

'I'll give you my phone number before we leave,' hissed Mia.

'Would you like a coffee, Jack?' said Cleo, her arms rubbing her shoulders. 'I'm getting cold.'

'Wouldn't mind at all,' he said.

'And if you don't mind me saying, I wouldn't leave your daughter with my son.'

'I keep forgetting,' mumbled Jack. 'She's only fourteen.'

'Martin!' bellowed Cleo. 'Leave that young girl alone. She's well under age. I'm running a respectable guest house. I want you to collect the dishes on the patio. Come on. You want food and board? Then do something to justify your presence on earth.'

Martin sullenly left them and went to the patio.

'Come on, love.' Cleo went across and put an arm round Mia. 'Don't trust my son an inch. He'll leave you pregnant with triplets and run off to South America. Come into the kitchen; we'll warm up with a coffee.'

Chapter 17

Upstairs, on the top floor of the house, Jean was sitting on the bed in Larry's room, an unmoveable object, her face heavily made up, red hair bright in the overhead lamp. Beryl was by the door, Larry on the chair at the small dressing table-cum-desk, his back to his wife.

'Please leave my room,' he said, not turning but viewing his wife in the mirror.

'I've come for some answers,' said Jean. 'And I'm not leaving before I get them. Is that too much to ask after thirty one years together?' She looked to Beryl. 'Please leave us. This is between me and my husband.'

'He wants you to go,' said Beryl.

'I do have ears,' said Jean. 'I don't need an interpreter. I think your room is down a floor.'

'I've said all I am going to say to you, Jean,' said Larry.

He would not turn to face her, as if that small movement would have admitted her right to be here and hear his explanation. Which hardly made sense to himself, let alone someone else. Its very fragility would not allow expression. What he was doing, who he had become.

As if he knew.

'I got your email about one o'clock,' she said. 'And since then I have travelled 200 miles for elucidation. Who is this woman you are having a liaison with?' She held up her hands to prevent a reply. 'No. Don't tell me. I wouldn't know her from Eve. Someone twenty years younger than you, I'm sure. The male menopause, isn't that what they call it? There you are, dear, well into middle age, hair very grey, belly straining at the waist band, but desperate to prove, that however else you've failed in life, you can still get it up.' She turned to Beryl. 'I'm sure you've bedded a few straining egos, Beryl. Is that your philanthropy? Though in this bright light, it's obvious you're just a smidgeon away from middle age yourself.'

'At least I don't need to dye my hair red,' exclaimed Beryl. 'And my tits haven't slipped to my waist.'

'Pay attention to her, listen to her coarseness, Larry. And protect me from the whore masquerading as your sister.'

'Leave this room,' said Larry between gritted teeth. 'I didn't ask you to come. I don't want you here.'

Beryl could just see herself in the mirror in front of Larry. She didn't look bad at all for her age. Yes, she'd put on weight but it was in all the right places. Men found the extra pounds attractive. But Jean was plump. No, fat. Say it how it is. All the fat round her belly and on her hippopotamus rump. And that stupid red colour of her hair, so obviously dyed. Make-up plastered on, lipstick colour to match her hair. How crude, how obvious! Was she hoping to tempt Larry back? Stupid old cow.

'Your bit of fluff will soon grow tired of you,' said Jean. 'Best act your age. Show some gumption for once in your life. We have a son in the United States. What are you going to tell him?'

'I have nothing to say to you,' said Larry. 'I've had nothing to say for ten years.'

'Now you're being nasty, for nastiness' sake. Petulant. A young body has you in its thrall. Like an old bull, all steamed up, but penned in. Take a look at yourself. Yes, in the mirror. You are on your way to total humiliation.'

'I've told you where I stand, Jean. Made it plain. I have left you. We are separated. Go away.'

'We have a son in common, dear. Thirty one years of memories. We have half shares in our house. Don't for one moment think I agree to sell up, or I'm going to buy you out. You can come back to live in our house, as you should, but you won't get a penny out of it.'

'You are a disgusting bitch!' Larry rose, turned and shook a fist at her. 'I should have left you a decade ago.'

He stormed from the room with his sister following him.

'Come to my room, Larry,' his wife heard her fading voice. 'Leave Jean there to stew.'

Cleo poured the coffee into three mugs. She was with Jack and Mia at the kitchen table, the worktops about them piled with dirty dishes, pots and oven trays. But Cleo had cleared the table to give an oasis of calm.

'What were you and Martin talking about, Mia?' she said, passing her a mug.

'Astronomy. I showed him Mizar in the Plough. It's a triple star through a telescope.'

'I find that hard to believe,' said Cleo. 'His main interests are weed, sex and money.' She put up a hand to correct herself. 'No. His only interests.'

'Did he proposition you?' said Jack.

'No.'

Cleo took a sip of coffee. She'd had a long day and was looking weary. And all this mess to clear away before bed. Then breakfast to be made for a full house in the morning. Jack wondered how old she was. A few years older than him, but wearing well, only a little make-up on her brown face, and a skim of orange lipstick. A good figure, well, she worked hard, non-stop from what he'd seen.

'I'll give him an ultimatum,' said Cleo. 'I will not have him sleeping with underage girls. Not here. Not anywhere, if I have a say in it.'

'I'll have more than a say,' hissed Jack. 'That's if I don't hit him with a pickaxe handle.'

'I don't need protection,' said Mia wearily. 'I can live my own life.' She was looking down into her coffee, keeping her eyes off the two adult guardians.

There was a flurry of footsteps above them, followed by raised voices.

'What's going on upstairs?' said Jack.

'Family row,' said Cleo. 'Larry, his missus and Beryl are up there.'

Jack said, 'He emailed his wife this afternoon, saying he wasn't coming back, that he'd been having an affair the last couple of months.'

Cleo spluttered her coffee about the table.

'Excuse me. Dreadful manners.' She stretched out to reach a kitchen roll, tore off a piece and wiped the table. 'Larry's shy as a mouse,' she said, finishing the wipe down and putting the tissue in the bin. 'I bet Jean asked him out on their first date, got his trousers down and told him how to do it.' She turned to Mia. 'Sorry, dear, if I am a little direct.'

'I do know the facts of life,' she said, without looking up.

'Larry hasn't been working for the last two months,' said Jack.

'You mean it's all a pretence, for our benefit? Going out in his suit?' Jack nodded. 'Well, well. It figures though. That's why Beryl wants me to cut his rate.'

'He's on half already,' said Jack.

'Beryl can strike a sharp bargain. Oh yes. She'd be queen of any souk.'

'Why?' said Jack. 'If you don't mind me asking...'

'Confidential,' she said. 'I've said too much. Mustn't drink. You're too easy to talk to.'

They were silent a while, drinking their coffee. Cleo was looking around at the dishes on the worktops, obviously planning what had to be done by the morning. Martin had brought in a trayful of crockery from the patio and gone back for more. Cleo had an active life, this place, her son, and all the palaver with Beryl. She was attractive. Animated, he could see the singer and dancer in her.

She was looking at him, he was looking at her. Mia was playing with bread crumbs on the table. One at a time. Beryl had kissed him and they had fixed up tomorrow. One at a time. Jack looked at his watch. Time to pack up. Mia had school tomorrow, she wouldn't be in bed till past ten thirty. And he was going for a blood test first thing in the morning.

His blood, pumping now, as he looked again at Cleo. She had risen, and picked up a pile of plates...

There was yelling from the garden, crockery breaking.

'What on earth is going on out there?' exclaimed Cleo.

Cleo raced out, followed by Jack. Mia, alone in the kitchen, tore off a piece of kitchen roll and scrawled her phone number on it. She put it in the pocket of her jeans and followed them out, curious to what was going on.

On the patio, Clyde had hold of George by the shoulders and was shaking him vigorously. George had a bloody nose and was trying to push him off.

'All day you've been following me!' shrieked Clyde. 'And now you've stolen my phone.'

'Break it up! Break it up!' yelled Cleo, forcing herself between them, trying to push them apart.

'He's a thief!' yelled Clyde. 'He's been on my tail all day long.'

He threw a punch which would have hit Cleo but Jack caught his arm and swung him round, pulling him away from George. Clyde staggered, almost falling over, catching himself on the table, which he almost toppled over, but Cleo ran in and caught it. She steadied the crockery, and pushed surviving dishes further in.

Jack took Clyde to a chair and dropped him in it.

'I've been up West all day.' George appealed to the onlookers, as he wiped blood off his nose on the back of his hand. 'I don't know anything about his phone.'

'If there is any more fighting,' ordered Cleo, 'I'm going to call the police. This is a respectable guest house.' She turned to Clyde and George. 'Behave or leave.'

'He started it!' exclaimed George. 'Thumped me on the nose, half strangled me.'

'You're a thief!' yelled Clyde. 'You have been following me. I saw you at the hospital... You've been in my room.'

'He's drunk, he's crazy,' exclaimed George, keeping well away from Clyde. 'I was sitting here, minding my own business, and out of the blue, he attacked me.'

'This your phone?' said Cleo.

She bent down to pick up a phone lying on the patio paving in a broken dish of salad. She passed it to Clyde. He looked at it, puzzled, pressed a couple of buttons, looked at the screen.

'It's mine,' he said sheepishly, then, remembering to be consistent, bellowed, 'He stole it, I tell you. He just dropped it. He has been following me all day.'

'Give it a rest, will you?' said George. 'Why on earth should I want to follow you? You own a goldmine?'

Jack had an arm on Clyde's shoulder, keeping him seated in the chair. He slid down beside him.

'Calm down, mate,' he said. 'Fighting won't help any. You've got your phone back. You may well have dropped it. You've been drinking, it was dark.'

'He has been following me, Jack,' said Clyde in a muted voice. 'I swear it.'

Cleo pushed George to the French windows. 'Best get you washed up. Let's go inside.'

'He's bonkers,' exclaimed George to those on the patio, 'I was just sitting there...' as Cleo ushered him into the lounge.

Jack went to a corner of the patio and brought back the patio broom. He swept around and under the table, pushing the damaged glass, a smashed salad bowl, knives, forks and serving utensils against the wall, out of the way. He put down the broom and began sorting the broken from the unbroken. Mia joined him.

'Be careful,' said Jack. 'There's some nasty shards.'

The patio light was on, there were just leavings on the table and scattered about. The barbecue was definitely over. He'd had hardly any time at the telescope.

'Start packing up the scope,' he said to Mia. 'I'll help in a mo'. I need a word with Clyde.'

'OK.' She nodded, understanding the necessity. And left.

Jack watched her off. She knew the drill, had done it often enough. He had no worries there. Jack turned to Clyde, almost a formless baggage, slumped in the chair. They were the only ones left outside. Jack took a seat next to him.

'You are Paul Blake, aren't you?' he said.

Clyde clutched Jack's arm. 'Please don't use that name. I haven't been him for seventeen years. Forget Paul Blake.'

Clyde was trembling, smelling strongly of booze. Trying to forget his pain with a whisky bottle, too recognisable for Jack. Clyde had secrets, Jack was curious. But leave it. He must get Mia home. He wondered where Beryl was. This turbulent house.

'It doesn't matter to me what you call yourself,' he said, a hand on Clyde's shoulder. 'It's obvious you've got hassles. Don't try to drink your way out of them.'

The last statement he knew to be useless advice, even as it escaped from his mouth. Once medicinal drinking seeped in, it dulls any willpower, listening to nothing but its own necessity to block out the world.

'I got to get back to Canada, Jack. Soon, soon as I can. I'm leaving in the morning. Gotta go, gotta go from here. If that devil follows me, I'll kill him for sure.'

Chapter 18

It was well past eleven when they got back home.

'Don't tell your mum I've kept you out this late,' said Jack.

'Don't worry.'

'Clean your teeth and go to bed. I've got to be up early for a blood test. So don't panic if I'm not here first thing. I'll be back in time for breakfast.'

'I've got to be up early too. You're not the only one.'

'What for?'

'I've got rehearsal. Our jazz quartet. At 8am. Last time I was late and they all had a go at me. I'm going to be first in tomorrow.'

'Get moving then. Get some sleep.'

Mia went to the bathroom. Jack made himself a cup of tea and considered the evening. Here so quiet, while Cleo was in the midst of a maelstrom. George and Clyde, two black guys spinning round each other like second rate boxers, Larry and his wife, the white tribe, throwing meta-phorical punches. He thought about Beryl, recalling the kiss on the patio. Definitely attractive, no denying her fleshiness and curves. She knew how to dress and make herself up. But what was she like really? Certainly had her claws in Cleo.

Wasn't that the way with relationships? You never get just the life and soul of the party, but all the hassles and torments of a person.

Cleo too. Attractive, but she was tied to Martin and to her bed and breakfast. Well, it couldn't always be so frantic.

Must have its calm days. Except she might not pay him, and if he had to take her to small claims court, that would kill any chances of anything else.

Could he never stop? Always weighing things up. Sex and money.

And now there was food, just to vary matters, every spoonful had to be considered twice. But sex trumped everything, every time.

At least Beryl supported her brother. A point in her favour. Loyalty. And she was coming round tomorrow evening. Don't expect too much. There will be no cottage with roses round the door, two kids on the swing. None of that.

Sex, plain old sex. And she was quite a bundle.

The alarm woke him at 6.30 am. He switched it off and jumped out of bed. He was never one for putting the clock on snooze. That way you never got up. He dressed and washed, cleaned his teeth. He mustn't eat at all, not even a cup of tea. The rule for the blood test was that he had to fast overnight, which was why he was going early. The clinic opened at 7 am and he'd be one of the first. That was convenient for work. He'd be done with in quarter of an hour and be back to breakfast with Mia.

Jack left the house at 6.45. It was chilly, but a brisk walk would clear the cobwebs and keep him warm. The sky was overcast, but just white cloud, which hopefully meant no rain so he could put down a little more sand and lay the concrete. And finish today. Then a week for the concrete to set, and come back for a day's work assembling the summerhouse.

And hopefully get paid.

Jack arrived at the clinic at 7 exactly. There were three in front of him. He took a numbered ticket, sat down and waited to be called. Another couple came and took tickets. How many of those seated here, waiting for a blood test, he wondered, were diabetics? Like him, getting the test early so they could have breakfast, as they'd had to fast beforehand.

Not a question you can ask of strangers. Besides, no one was talkative this time in the morning. That man though, bulky, a large gut, arms like fat clubs. He'd place a bet there. Or he could have something else entirely. Plenty of other ailments that gave clues in the blood stream.

Was this going to be a regular date?

Quite possibly. Unless he could cure himself by eating decent food, and so get his body's insulin working like it should. All in his hands, Dr Aziz had told him. Cure yourself or roll downhill.

Cut out bread and potatoes. Eat salad. What on earth was he going to have for lunch today? He was a builder, not an office worker. He had sand and concrete to heave. That couldn't be done on lettuce and carrots.

His number came on the screen. Jack walked past reception and into the clinic area. And was done in five minutes. A tiny tube of blood had been taken.

What were its secrets?

Mia was up when he got home. She'd showered and had breakfast on the table: muesli with milk and banana. He ate it and was still hungry, knowing there were two slices of bacon in the fridge. He was tempted and knew he would have fried them if Mia wasn't here.

He spread peanut butter on a slice of wholemeal bread.

'What am I going to have for lunch?' he said.

'What do you normally have?'

'Two cheese sandwiches, made with four slices of bread.'

'White bread,' she added contemptuously. 'Now we've got wholemeal. Make it three, and a banana.'

'OK,' he said reluctantly. Then added, 'You're not contacting that Martin, are you?'

'No,' she said. 'He's not my sort.'

'He must be ten years older than you.'

'That too.'

Mia left the kitchen. Jack wondered about her, the two of them conspiring at the telescope. Martin of all people; he'd heard nothing good of him.

Mia put her head round the kitchen door. She had her backpack on.

'Gotta go. Twenty to eight. Can't be late. I am going to be the first in for the music rehearsal.'

She left. He heard her skipping down the stairs. Jack made up his sandwiches and set off for work himself. Not knowing that his daughter had left her phone number in Martin's tent.

Chapter 19

Jack took out the shovel and rake from his van. That's all he needed, along with the wheelbarrow, for the next hour or so. It was quarter to eight, an early start. He could do half an hour's work before breakfast. Not that he was hungry, but he wanted a word with Beryl.

He locked the van and walked the dozen yards to the drive where the remnants of hardcore and sand were in the cubic sacks, along with the cement and the cement mixer that would certainly be needed in a few hours.

The wheelbarrow wasn't there.

Everything else was. He hadn't put it in the van last night because he didn't want the wheelbarrow rattling around with his telescope when he drove home. And now it was gone. What a pain! There was another at his lock-up which he'd have to go and collect. He couldn't work without one.

And then he noticed a spade in the sand. Not his spade either. And the level of the cubic metre pack of sand was lower. Someone was working. Had to be Larry; he'd have the wheelbarrow. He must have borrowed Cleo's spade to load the sand.

Not totally sure, but hoping so, he wended his way down the alley along the side of the house. Once out on the patio, he could see Larry with the wheelbarrow at the site. That was a relief. Wheelbarrows were cheap enough but it would be a hassle to get his other one.

As he crossed the lawn, Jack saw heaps of sand on the workings. Larry was raking them flat. That must be Cleo's rake too, he thought.

'I'm impressed,' he said at the site, hands on hips looking at the heaps of sand and those already raked flat.

'The apprentice has done an hour's work before the boss got in, sir,' said Larry with a smart salute.

'Trying to show me up, eh?'

Larry leaned on the rake. He was wearing the same clothes as he wore at the barbecue: dark blue trousers and a pink shirt. His shoes were patent leather, most unsuitable for working in. But Jack didn't want to start the day lecturing Larry on appropriate dress. If Larry chose to ruin his clothing and shoes that was his lookout. He had told him about them yesterday.

'I slept in the tent last night,' said Larry, indicating Martin's tent. 'And the sun woke me early. So I thought I might as well get working. If I went in the house to change, the wife might attack me.' He clutched his neck in a mock throttle. 'She slept in my room, you know, waiting for me. Fat chance.'

Jack attempted to catch up with the room swapping.

'You could've slept in her room,' he said.

'Locked,' he said. 'The cow stole my room. I should've called the cops on her.'

'I don't think they'd been a lot of help.'

'It's a liberty,' went on Larry. 'If I'd bundled her out, she could've had had me for assault.'

Jack had no wish to take sides in a domestic dispute. It had been musical rooms last night, though one place was spare, or was it?

'If you slept in the tent,' he said warily, 'then where did Martin sleep?'

'With Beryl,' said Larry, going back to the raking.

Jack contemplated the new information. Well, well, Beryl and Martin. That was a shake up of his dreams. She was of course a free woman, as he was a free man, with no obligations but a dinner tonight.

'I wouldn't have thought Martin was her sort,' he said, as calmly as he could.

'She's not fussy, my sister. Doesn't like to sleep on her own.'

So I'm lined up for tonight, thought Jack. Last night, Martin's turn. Did he really fancy dinner? No, sex, let's get it straight. Nothing but sex. No relationship, nowhere to go.

'I'll get some sand,' he said.

Jack set off with the wheelbarrow and shovel, wondering why he was so peeved. He had no claims on Beryl. She was an adult, he was an adult. A male thing, he realised. A woman who slept round was a slut, a man who did it was a bit of a lad. Well, he'd like to be one, but his success rate was low on the gigolo grading.

Just as well, he thought as he began filling the wheelbarrow with sand. Ageing Don Juans are pathetic, trying to hold back the years like King Canute in the surf. OK, he wasn't old, though diabetes made him feel aged. And had some would-be Don Juan in him, opportunity granted, didn't most guys? But Don Juans had no interest in romance. They used it as a ruse to fill their bed. As for himself, taking his Don Juan complex out of the equation, he wanted more than sex. All the well worn cornball stuff, hearts and flowers, valentine cards. The cottage with roses round the door.

What a pathetic romantic!

Cleo was more his thing, and seemed to be free. Except she had that dreadful son. Always a snag. Something to sully the dreamy vision. Though Martin might head off to South America or Timbuktu, or anywhere a long way off, where he could be eaten by a crocodile.

Having polished off Martin, he wondered if the fact that her son slept with Beryl would bother Cleo?

Why did she have to know? Who was going to tell her?

That was Don Juan talking. Though he could hardly blame Martin, considering. Just take care with Beryl. She could be ruthless, as he'd gathered from Cleo, though not the full picture. And only one side of the tale. Best not make an enemy of her. If he went ahead with the dinner, she'd discard him soon enough.

Take one day at a time. Dinner and bed. Or bed and dinner. Whichever way it happened. Or neither. Never forgetting, that was an option too.

She might chuck him.

Jack chuckled, as he wheeled the full barrow back, a man of the world once more, whatever that meant. It probably didn't include type 2 diabetes. OK, a somewhat shop soiled, slightly damaged in transit man of the world, but with a good sense of humour and a 150 millimetre reflector, as if he were composing copy for a dating ad.

The imperfect seeking the perfect. Contact me with photo.

As he came into the site, Larry stopped raking and called:

'The pegs in that form are coming out.'

He pointed out one of the wooden sides, put in to contain the concrete. 'It's too high.'

Jack left the wheelbarrow of sand. He knelt down by the plank Larry had indicted. And yes, it was high, two of the pegs holding it bent over.

'Someone at the barbecue must've kicked it,' said Larry.

'More than kicked it,' murmured Jack. 'Teach me to set the telescope so close. My fault.' He shrugged. 'We'll have to re-level that plank, so we get an even depth of concrete.' He tipped out the sand from the wheelbarrow into the filling base. 'I'll get the spirit level and hammer from my van, and a last load of sand. Soon put that right. Well spotted.'

Jack set off for the van with the wheelbarrow. Wouldn't take long to re-level the plank. As well to check anyway. Not a problem, as with Larry's early start they were ahead this morning. In the drive, Jack shovelled the sand into the barrow leisurely. Mustn't work too hard. That's the first law. He had taken his tablet this morning, but hadn't the greatest confidence in its efficacy. Too soon to know.

In the meantime, pace the work and eat properly. His lunch was one slice of bread less, replaced by a banana, and wholemeal bread too. He was bound to slip from this moral excellence.

The wheelbarrow full, Jack went to his van for the gear needed to level the form: a hammer, a long plank, and his spirit level. The plank and spirit level, Jack found straight off. But he couldn't find a hammer. A club hammer or claw hammer, either would do. It was just for bashing in the pegs to hold the form in, once it was re-levelled. The hammers should be on top. He was always using hammers. He'd used the club hammer yesterday, banging in the pegs, and the claw hammer too. So where on earth were they? Had he put them back in the van? All these timber pieces, saws, rolls of wire, boxes of screws, his portable work bench, paint sheets, step ladder. A set square he thought he'd lost. Everything but hammers. They were smallish items and could easily be hidden under a bucket or his workbench, or the host of bits and pieces filling the back of his van. But the two of them?

Jack got inside the van and scrabbled about. So frustrating, he had had them yesterday, used the club hammer to bang in the forms and pegs. Larry had used the claw hammer.

That's what happens when you think about sex all day. You lose things. You do things in a dream, and can't remember later. They must be here somewhere. He took out his workbench, the step ladder, several buckets, a toolbox, two trestles and various oddments of wood, which should be thrown out, and put them on the pavement. But no hammers.

When did he last have them? He distinctly remembered using the club hammer for putting the forms and pegs in. OK. Did he put it away at the end? Surely he had. He wasn't marking everything off on a checklist, but he'd put away everything that was lying about.

Not here. Must be somewhere. Where?

He searched again where he'd already searched. And then gave up. They had to be here, he was just overlooking them. They'd turn up. Probably in three months when he'd bought new ones. Such a waste of time. He must give the van a good clear out, just keep with him what he needed. The trouble was, he was never sure, going from job to job, what would be needed. So he ended up keeping too much, just in case.

Jack settled for a wooden mallet. It would work almost as well, he wasn't banging in nails. But it was so infuriating losing two hammers. Not one even, but two. He'd had them both a long time, the club hammer, a faithful tool, when you wanted to give something a hefty clout.

He loaded the gear on the pavement back into the van. And locked it. What a stupid runaround, he'd hardly done any work. Larry was showing him up. Tomorrow, he'd give the van a clear out.

Jack put the mallet, plank and spirit level on top of the sand in the wheelbarrow and headed back.

'Took your time,' said Larry.

'Couldn't find my hammers,' said Jack, 'I've looked everywhere for them. But never mind, the mallet is almost as good. You've changed your shirt.'

Larry had put on the grubby t-shirt he'd been wearing yesterday.

'Had it in the tent,' said Larry. 'I thought why ruin a good shirt.'

'Not unless you're made of money.'

He wondered why it had taken him an hour to change his shirt. But Larry was an office worker, with lots of shirts. No, he was a pretend office worker, or had been, everyone knew what was what now. Unemployed, amongst the great unwashed. All the more reason to look after decent clothes.

'Why is a plank called a form?' said Larry.

Jack shrugged. 'That's only when it's holding in concrete.'

'Forming it,' said Larry snapping his fingers.

'Sounds right.'

It was too early to discuss the meaning of words. And he was still irritated at having misplaced two hammers. If he couldn't find them, he would have to buy new ones. What a waste of cash!

He and Larry worked on the form which had come out of place, and checked the others. With the spirit level and cross plank they got all four forms level. Jack hammered the pegs in with the mallet. There must be a graveyard where lost tools end up. A yard full of hammers, saws, drills and buckets of nails and screws.

'Beryl said she's going over your place for dinner tonight,' said Larry.

The complications of a gigolo, thought Jack. All lies and secrets. The less people who knew the better, especially as he had an eye on Cleo.

'Yes, Beryl's coming over,' said Jack. 'Don't know what I'm going to cook.' Adding facetiously, 'Does she like beans on toast?'

'Beryl is fussy about food. She's a good cook. My wife belongs to a local choir. When there's a choir practice, Beryl comes over with a load of food and prepares a meal.

Cordon bleu.' He kissed his fingers. 'Multi-talented is Beryl. Not just sex.' He winked at Jack.

'I need to have a word with her. Perhaps she'd cook if I bought the ingredients. Do you think?'

'Look! A Holly Blue.' Larry pointed out a butterfly skittering across the lawn and then onto the vegetable garden. 'First I've seen this year.'

Jack took half a glance, his mind was not on butterflies.

'There was a heath at the back of the house,' went on Larry watching the flight. 'As a teenager I'd be over there with a net. Beryl, she's ten years younger than me, from when she was about 9, she'd join me. Had her own net. She was ace at catching them. Fast. She'd be after them like a sprinter from the gun, stop once the butterfly had settled. Draw in closer, slowly like a cat. And pounce. She was good, better than me. Better than me at everything. My sister.'

Larry sighed. 'Over twenty years ago, when I was last out with a net. Jean, the one who must be obeyed, didn't like me killing them. They're only insects, I'd tell her. You'd kill a wasp. But she wouldn't listen. Everyone swats flies, puts down ant killer, who wouldn't stomp on a cockroach? It's painless for them, they don't have a brain. You put the butterfly in a jar, along with a little ethyl acetate on cotton wool. Close the lid. They were dead by the time we got home. There, we'd dry them out on tissue paper. And the next day, I'd stick a single pin through the thorax. I've got a dozen racks of butterflies, twenty four in each. There's not much I want from home, but I want my butterflies. Those were the days, out on the heath with the net, me and Beryl. I used to so enjoy looking up the specimens in the book, writing out the labels. And sticking them neatly on the board with the pin.'

Jack was only half listening to Larry's dream of past butterflies. One more load of sand needed. He'd been preoccupied by food and Beryl. Though the thought of

Beryl darting round with a net on the heath, in shorts and t-shirt, could well liven his interest in lepidoptera.

Forget Beryl on the heath. How was he going to arrange a meal tonight? He must talk to her, explain his lack of cooking skills. He should learn to cook. Like Dr Aziz said.

What was easy, apart from beans on toast?

Ice cream and peaches for pudding. That was simple. It was the main dish that floored him. Salad. He could handle that. Make it colourful, Mia had told him. What with it? Rice. No, that always ended up sticky, stuck to the pot. Steak. That was pricey, but if you can't cook that's the way. Grill it. Couscous. That wasn't difficult. Mia had made some once, just poured boiling water over it.

Melon for starters! That was ingenious. So easy, just take the pips out.

He almost bounced with the wheelbarrow, delighted with himself, it might be expensive, but he had a menu, more or less. He'd go off and buy the ingredients after work. This cooking lark could be interesting. And he could talk to her about butterflies. Tell her he'd seen a Holly Blue.

Chapter 20

Jack washed his hands under the patio tap. He had thought not to go into breakfast today, as watching the rest of them eating their full English fry ups wasn't good for him. But he wanted a word with Beryl, mind you, not with everyone listening, just a word was all that he wanted. Tell her to pop into the garden before work, so he could fix things for tonight.

He must tidy the van, find the hammers. Forget hammers. Think of sex and melon.

At the table, along with Jack, were Larry, George, Clyde and Jean. Larry had got as far away from Jean as he could. She was staring at him sternly but he was making every effort not to look at her. Hard work, thought Jack.

Martin was coming in and out from the kitchen in a cook's hat and a long white apron, tied at the waist and looped round his neck. Jack was impressed how he'd got all that hair under the hat.

'My mother says I must earn my keep,' he said cheerfully, as he placed out a platter of toast. 'She had me in the kitchen at seven sharp. I never knew there was such an hour.'

'Good for you,' said Jean primly. 'I'm often in the office by seven. Get two hours undisturbed work done before the others get in.'

'I'm a night bird myself,' said George. 'If there wasn't breakfast on the table awaiting me, I'd still be in bed.' He looked at his watch. 'Beryl is having a lie in, I notice.'

'After that barbecue, with all the booze,' said Larry, 'I'm surprised we're all here.' To Clyde, he said, 'You were well tanked.'

'I only drink on social occasions,' said Clyde. 'And sometimes, I go too far.'

'You seem to have a lot of social occasions,' said George.

Clyde glared at him, was about to respond but instead attacked the toast. Martin brought in a tray of bacon, Cleo followed with one of fried eggs.

'Eat up, everyone,' she said. 'And you, Jack. Join in. Payment for the telescope session.'

'Thank you,' he said, wondering whether she was softening him up for the time when she wouldn't be paying him. But today was today, forget tomorrow. He weighed up the food on the table. Not too much. All the rules. The eggs and bacon were both fried. But the toast was wholemeal as well as white. Could he skip the bacon? It was so inviting.

'Can you give Beryl a call, love?' said Cleo to Martin.

'Sure.'

Martin left them. Cleo took a seat at the table.

'So what's everyone doing today?' she said.

'I'm going home,' said Jean. 'Back to work. Unlike some I know.'

She was in a white shirt and navy trousers, the same uniform that Beryl wore for work, which made Jack wonder about Beryl sleeping in. Perhaps the effects of a night of lovemaking with Martin, who was awfully cheerful and clean, so unlike the vagabond who'd arrived yesterday morning.

'I've wasted more than enough time here,' went on Jean. 'I am not one who stays where I am not wanted. My husband doesn't care to talk to me, he has another bird in hand, so I shall no longer humiliate myself by sticking around.'

Jack was watching Larry, who was concentrating on his food as if it were a delicate operation, cutting the bacon precisely, forking a piece and dipping it into the egg yolk.

One slice of bacon wouldn't kill him, thought Jack. He took one. Oh why not, in for a penny in for a pound. And took another.

'I'm off too,' said George. 'The British Museum nearly killed me. All those stairs and the floors the size of aircraft hangars. The place I always go to, the mummies. You can't help thinking there's a body wrapped up in all that bandage, dead for three thousand years...'

Martin returned.

'Her door's locked,' he said. 'I called but she didn't respond.'

'Could be in the shower,' said Cleo. 'I'll go. She always has breakfast before work.'

Cleo left the room. Martin sat down at the table.

'What are you up to today?' said Jack.

'Me?' he exclaimed, as if surprised to be included. 'Well, first me and mum have to clear up after breakfast. Then she wants me to help with the shopping. That's my morning fully timetabled. I'm not sure about the afternoon.'

Larry said, 'Jack and I will be laying concrete. Isn't that so, Jack?'

'It is,' he said. 'We are all set. There's a good level of hardcore and sand. The forms are at the right level, so full steam ahead with the cement mixer.'

'It's so satisfying,' said Larry. 'Completing something. I fully get it. Office work just goes on forever, more buying, more selling, accounts and accounts, meetings upon meetings, managerial assessments, year on, year out. Nothing is ever finished. You wonder why you are there, what you are achieving. But we are making a base for a summerhouse, which could be around for fifty years. Wouldn't you say, Jack?'

Jack noted that Larry was completely ignoring his wife. Refusing to even look at her. But it was fake, his energy and spark too high, purposely, for her benefit. Demonstrating he had no need of her, and his decrying of office work was totally to attack her useless working life.

'The summerhouse won't last fifty years,' said Jack. 'It's only wood. But the base could be intact for a century or more. Not that I'm giving a hundred year guarantee.'

'None of us would be around to collect,' said George.

Cleo popped her head into the lounge.

'Could I have a word, Jack?' She beckoned him.

'What, Beryl stuck in the bath!' chortled George.

Jack left them at the table and followed Cleo into the hall. She walked rapidly down the hallway, and almost trotted up the stairs. Jack wondered what this was about. Some repair?

On the landing, she put a finger to her lips, he could see she was shaking.

'What is it?' he said.

'She's dead. Beryl. Dead,' said Cleo, her hands going to her cheeks. 'No answer when I knocked on the door. I went in, with my key. And found her lying on the floor, in her dressing gown, her head smashed in.'

Jack, thrown by the image of Beryl, by Cleo's distress, put a hand on the wall for support. Dead, Beryl, the one who'd been occupying his thoughts the last hour, who was coming over this evening. Beryl lying on the floor with her head smashed in.

'We must call the police,' he said mechanically. The words one always says when the worst happens. A head smashed in means murder. He was already considering who might have done it.

'We must call the police,' he repeated.

'You don't understand,' she whispered, putting a hand on his arm. 'I thought of killing her myself. She's been blackmailing me. I thought of how to do it. When, where. And now she's dead. They'll arrest me, Jack. When one of those at the table,' she pointed down the stairs, 'has done it.'

'Who?'

'I don't know.' She was clutching her scalp, curly hair leaking between her fingers. 'Jack, Jack, if we tell them before the police arrive, they'll all run off. Including the murderer. And I'll be arrested.'

He was about to say she wouldn't be, but it occurred to him she well might be. Blackmail was a strong motive.

'I'll phone the police,' he said. 'But we won't tell the others anything has happened. OK?' She nodded, grateful he'd taken over. 'I'll make something up. A leak in the upstairs toilet.'

'I can't face them,' she said.

'Go in the kitchen, make coffee,' he said. 'Lots of it. And I'd best take a quick shifty at Beryl before I phone the cops. So I know what to say.'

She nodded, turned, and led him along the hallway. She opened the end door, and stepped aside.

'I don't need a second look,' she said. 'The first one will last me a lifetime.'

Jack took a deep breath, stomach turning over in trepidation. This had to be faced. He stepped cautiously into the room. And immediately saw her, lying flat out, by the bed, on her front in her short dressing gown, blood seeping into the carpet from her head. He went closer, breathing heavily, and knelt down, taking care not to touch her. Beryl's skull had caved in with the blow, there were bits of brain amidst blood and bone.

He stepped back, and out of the room, struggling to keep his food down.

'Lock the door,' he said. 'I'll phone the cops.'

Chapter 21

'So what's up with Beryl?' said George, dipping toast into his egg.

'She's in the bath,' said Cleo, 'dyeing her hair. She'll be about half an hour.'

Jack could see that her eyes were welling, an instant away from tears.

'What colour?' demanded Jean.

'Red,' said Cleo, blinking rapidly. 'I'll get the coffee.'

And left the room.

'Why would she dye her hair red,' declared Jean, 'if not to spite me?' She glared around the table, her red hair neat and curled. 'What do you think, Larry?'

Larry held a piece of forked sausage in mid air as he spoke.

'My sister can dye her hair any colour she wishes.'

'He speaks to me! He speaks to me,' exclaimed Jean. 'You are my witnesses. Did he not address a sentence to me?'

Larry gazed at the piece of sausage as if it had a message for him.

'Why did Cleo want you?' said George to Jack.

'There's a leak in the first floor toilet,' he said. 'Nothing serious, I've put a bucket under it. I'll fix it after breakfast.'

'Can we still use it?' said Clyde.

'You can,' said Jack, full knowing that if anyone went up there would be no leak or bucket.

The police had told him they'd be here shortly. However long that was. He had lost interest in his food, the bacon was too flesh coloured, his stomach having other distractions, but he felt he had to look like he was here to eat. That all was regular, nothing had changed. Jack took a piece of toast from the platter and buttered it, taking his time, covering the sides and corners completely. Then took a portion of marmalade, delicately drew off the plastic lid and smeared it slowly on the bread. It was more like an art project than preparing food to eat.

'I wonder what her people at work will think,' said Jean, 'when she turns up this morning with bright-red hair.'

'Tarty,' said George. 'No offence intended,' he said to Jean, 'it's just with younger women, no offence, it says I am available.'

'First I've heard of it,' said Martin.

'She's always available. That one! No need for traffic lights,' exclaimed Jean crunching on a piece of toast.

'We shouldn't criticise guests at the table,' said Martin.

They all looked to him in surprise, his moral stricture so unlikely. But who knew him really?

'Basic good manners,' he said.

'What a valiant knight you are, defending the tart you were screwing all night,' declared Jean. 'Don't think we couldn't hear you.'

'I don't think that at all,' said Martin. 'In fact, I don't care.'

'My sister is a grown up,' said Larry. 'Who she sleeps with is her affair.'

'Right on,' said Martin.

'And there's my husband who will defend his sister to the hilt. Let her screw an army and he will say, she's grown up, it's her business. How mature of you!'

'I think we should talk about something else,' said Larry. 'I am sure our family affairs are boring everyone.'

'Not at all,' said George. 'I'm intrigued. You two splitting up. You, Larry, defending your sister while your wife hates her like poison. I wonder what your Christmas dinners are like.'

'Dreadful,' said Larry.

George laughed. 'No one wants to pull a cracker with anyone!'

Jack took a bite of the marmalade toast. It tasted like cardboard, the jam too sugary, acid. He put down the slice with the single bit out of it, and, with an effort, chewed what was in his mouth, though wanting to spit it out, his stomach rumbling a warning. He was trying to observe the others at the table, to ascertain which of them knew Beryl was dead. But his observation skills were dulled by his stomach and the vision in the bedroom.

'You're quiet,' said Larry to Jack.

He tried a smile, it felt false, on a near paralysed face.

'I'm thinking about work,' he said. 'How much concrete we'll need. If we'll have enough hardcore and sand for the mix.'

Cleo came in with a large cafetière of coffee.

'I'll bring another,' she said, placing it in the centre of the table. 'Don't stint yourselves.'

'Are you keeping a breakfast for Beryl?' said Larry.

'Yes, I am,' she said. 'There'll be plenty for her. I'm keeping it warm. Don't worry.'

She left the room. Jack guessed she was holding back her tears for the kitchen. He was feeling sick himself. Dare he try some coffee?

'I'm looking forward to our new redhead,' said George.

'Until she completely dries her hair, it will be disappointing,' said Jean. 'But then that's par for the course with Beryl. She majored in disappointment.'

'Cut it out,' said Martin sharply.

'Oh, then she didn't disappoint you, young man?'

He glared at her across the table. 'You are a cow,' he said.

'And who was it said no criticising guests at the table?'

120

'Mine is a factual statement. You are a cow, honestly and truthfully.'

Larry said, 'Please don't insult bovine grazers, Martin. What have they ever done to you?'

George chuckled. 'I wish I could play,' he said. 'But I'm not a relative, and haven't slept with anyone in the family.'

'You're welcome to my wife,' said Larry.

George laughed outrageously, swinging back and forth. Jean threw down her fork and rose.

'You are a gathering of swine!' she exclaimed, and swept from the room.

George clapped.

'More! More!' he called after her. 'Please don't leave without an encore.'

But she had gone. Jack wondered whether she was going up to the first floor toilet. It was unlikely that she'd notice the lack of leak or bucket, or even care if she did. He considered going to the toilet himself, and sticking his fingers down his throat. But he might miss something here, not that his concentration was the greatest.

'Tell me,' said George. 'Who does your wife hate most, Larry, you or your sister?'

'Definitely my sister,' he said. 'Hated her from the off. It's a trial to be in the room with the pair of them.'

'The Red Headed-League!' said George. He sniggered. 'Isn't that a short story?'

'Arthur Conan Doyle,' muttered Clyde. 'A Sherlock Holmes tale.'

'I'd forgotten you were in the room,' said George. 'Nice to hear from you. Phone working properly?'

Clyde glared at him, didn't reply, and took a sip of coffee.

Cleo came in with another cafetière which she placed in the centre of the table.

'Is Jean all right?' she said. 'The way she rushed past me...'

'Same as always,' said Larry. 'Don't worry. Somewhat uptight. Somewhat fraught. But she's leaving us, you'll be pleased to know.'

'She was an unexpected guest, turning up like that,' said Cleo. She looked around the table. 'Everybody happy?'

'Sit down and eat, Mum,' said Martin. 'It's all getting cold.'

'There's something I must do first,' said Cleo. 'Back in a mo.' And left them.

Martin blew out his cheeks. 'Is it always like this here?'

'Normally quite civilised,' said George. 'Even a little boring. Well, it was yesterday. But Jean has livened things up for us. And you had fun with Beryl last night.'

'Mind your own business.'

'Touchy, touchy.' George held up a hand. 'Good luck to you is all I'm saying. I'm sure none of us would say no to Beryl.'

'I don't like your foul mouth,' said Larry. 'Keep my sister off the agenda.'

'She's the one missing at the table.'

'Along with his wife,' said Martin. 'Who hates his sister.' He thought for a second. 'But you're right, Larry. Too much about Beryl. What's the weather forecast for today?'

'Aren't West Ham playing tonight?' said George. And laughed.

Someone was bundling down the stairs with what sounded like a suitcase. Must be Jean, in a hurry to leave, thought Jack.

There was a long ring on the door bell. And then another.

Chapter 22

All the residents were seated in the lounge, on the sofa, armchairs and hardback chairs. The room had not quite ceased to function as the dining room, as they'd been ordered by the police to leave everything on the table. No clearing away was to be done. For maybe ten minutes, they'd been left with a police constable standing at the door to the hallway.

In that interval, following the police, crime scene operatives had arrived. There was lots of tramping up and down the stairs. George had tried to go out, but had been politely ordered to sit down. He'd noted a uniformed police woman at the foot of the stairs, the upper floors now out of bounds.

'May I have your attention, please.'

The voice came from a youngish, plain clothes Asian detective in a smart dark grey suit with a pale blue shirt and dark blue tie. A tall slim woman was by his side in navy trousers and shiny leather jacket.

The residents turned to him. Jean had her suitcase with her; she'd been about to leave when the police arrived, and was now in the lounge with the others. Jack was relieved that he no longer had to keep up the deception of normality. The object had been fulfilled, to keep everyone here until the police arrived.

There had been a few pointed remarks from the residents that he and Cleo knew all along that Beryl was dead, but the presence of the policeman had quelled further discussion.

'I am Detective Sergeant Fayyad Kamani,' said the man addressing them. 'And this is my colleague Detective Constable Hayley Amis.'

'Hello,' said the tall woman.

'As you are all aware, there's been a murder in this house. Beryl Taylor is the victim. A most brutal murder in an upstairs bedroom. We'd like you all to stay for the next few hours. If you really have a pressing engagement that can't be cancelled, then talk to me or my colleague. But please realise the first hours after a murder are the most important. Memories are fresh, the murderer has had less time to prepare his or her story or to remove evidence. So please, no trivial excuses for leaving. We wish to question all of you. This is preliminary questioning; you will all be required to give full statements at the police station. We'll also need to fingerprint everyone and take a DNA sample for elimination purposes. The samples will be destroyed after the investigation. You are not allowed upstairs as the crime scene investigators are busy there. In fact, you are confined to this room for the time being. Please excuse any inconvenience. Any questions?'

Fayyad looked around the room. Jack knew him from school. He bumped into Fayyad from time to time, both working locally.

Jack said, 'I suppose that means I can't work in the garden.'

'Sorry, but the house and garden are all part of the crime scene.'

'Any idea when I'll be able to get back to work?'

Fayyad shrugged. 'A day or two. I can't say exactly. Sorry.' His eyes tracked the room. 'Any other questions?'

'How did she die?' asked Larry.

'I'm not at liberty to say at the moment. Sorry,' said Fayyad. 'Anyone else with a question?' No one replied. 'A CSI investigator will take you one at time for fingerprinting and a DNA sample. It's not painful and only takes a minute or two. And we'll start our interviews with...' He took a notebook from his jacket pocket. 'Let me see.' He perused the page. 'Martin Dickens. Who's that?'

'Me,' called Martin. He was seated on the arm of a sofa. He had taken off the apron and cook's hat, his Afro billowing.

'If you'd like to follow me and DC Amis. The interviews will take place in the TV room.'

Martin followed Fayyad down the hallway, past the kitchen and the downstairs toilet. A police woman in uniform stood at the foot of the stairs. Up the stairs, on the landing, there were a number of people of indeterminate sex, covered in white crime scene gear from head to foot.

Fayyad led them into the TV room. It was a medium sized room with a sofa, two armchairs and several hardback chairs, and a large flat screen TV. The window had Venetian blinds through which could be seen the drive and people coming and going, in crime scene gear, from vehicles in the road.

Hayley closed the blinds and shut the door.

Fayyad indicated an armchair.

'Please sit down, Mr Dickens. Or may I call you Martin?'

'Martin is fine.' He sat down.

Fayyad and Hayley sat opposite on a sofa with a coffee table in front.

'Let's find out who you are, Martin.'

Hayley had opened her notebook and was ready with a pen to take notes.

'Cleo Dickens is my mother,' said Martin. 'I'm 22 years old. My dad is Ghanaian, making me three quarters black if you are any good at fractions. Never met my father. Mum tells me he was a dancer, and danced away, we don't know where.'

'How long have you been living here?'

'I'm back from Caracas, Venezuela. Arrived here yesterday morning. I was in South America for two years, mostly in Venezuela. I did some English teaching and bar work.'

'What made you come back?'

'Life's tough in Venezuela with the government and everything. The English teaching dried up. I just had enough money for a flight back. Wanted to see my mum. She's all I've got. Family, you know.'

'You are the last known person to have seen Beryl Taylor alive,' said Fayyad. 'You know that?'

'I didn't kill her, if that's what you are saying. Why should I? I only met her yesterday.'

'Tell me about meeting her.'

'Like I said, I arrived yesterday morning. Jet lagged. The place was full. Mum said the only place for me to sleep was a tent in the garden. Well, it's spring, not too bad. And only for sleeping. And I slept in some real dens in Caracas, I can tell you.'

'So how did you meet Beryl,' said Fayyad a little impatiently.

Martin smiled at him.

'I was getting to that. There was a barbecue last night, Jack, that's the builder, came back with his telescope. Quite a little party we had. Beryl and I got talking. And, you know how it is, I went to her room and stayed the night.'

'What time did you leave?'

'Mum called me at quarter to seven. I washed and dressed and was down in the kitchen by seven.'

'Let's be a little more precise. This is important. What time did you leave Beryl's room?'

'I'd say five to seven, give or take a minute or two. And she was fine. I gave her a kiss, and she told me she'd be up at seven thirty for a shower.'

'And you never went back to the room?'

'No. I worked with Mum setting the table, making the breakfast, serving it. And then I sat down to eat it. Never went upstairs again, after I left Beryl.'

'What do you know about her?'

'Not a lot. We didn't talk much. I just know what Mum told me when we were getting breakfast ready. She's an auditor, been staying here three days a week for about six months. Has a house somewhere up north. Can't remember where. And has some hold on my mum. Blackmail I think. I know she was staying here free, and Mum didn't like that. Can't afford it. And she got her brother half rate, that's Larry. Mum said Beryl was squeezing her dry. Don't tell her I told you. I just figured you'd find out anyway.'

'Did you kill her, Martin?'

'What! You trying to hang this one on me? I don't believe it. I only met her yesterday. What would I get out of it?'

'You said she had her hooks in your mother,' said Fayyad. 'Did you do it for her? Or maybe you are in it together?'

Martin slapped back in the chair and gazed up at the ceiling.

'I don't believe what I am hearing. The first young black guy you come across, he's the guilty party. Got to be. And mum, she's half black. So in it together. Case solved.'

'Beryl died somewhere between, let's say 6.50 and when we were called at 8.31. You were there at the beginning of that window.'

'I didn't kill her.'

'You've only your mother for an alibi.'

'She didn't kill her. Now find the white man who did.'

Chapter 23

'What do you think?' said Fayyad to Hayley.

They were in the TV room alone, having sent Martin back to join the others in the lounge.

'He has to be in the frame,' she said. 'The last known person to see her alive. He has to be hot.'

'The motive must be his mother, Beryl was blackmailing her. So dutiful son, just home from South America, wants to get in her good books, eliminates the blackmailer.'

'I can't think of any other motive he'd have,' said Hayley. 'There's no evidence of robbery.'

'No,' he said. 'I am bothered though.'

'By what?'

'It would be one hell of a callous act. He sleeps with her. We don't know who seduced whom. Besides the point. But he stays the night, makes love. At what point did he decide to kill her?'

'I see what you are getting at,' said Hayley. 'But psychopaths aren't sentimental. It could even be that while he was seducing her he'd decided to kill her. And thought to himself, why not make love first.' She waved a significant finger at him. 'It would be more satisfying than afterwards.'

'How cynical you are, Hayley.'

'We've met too many bad 'uns,' she said. 'It pays to think the worst.'

'I suppose he might have tried to persuade her, between bouts, to let up on his mother...'

'And she wasn't giving an inch.'

'I'm trying to make the young man slightly nicer,' said Fayyad. 'Defending the male sex.'

Hayley laughed. 'Down from one hundred per cent beast to ninety nine point nine!'

'Big beast or lesser beast, time of death is crucial,' said Fayyad. 'The phone call to us was timed at 8.31. If Martin killed her, he could've done it any time in the night. If he didn't...'

'If he didn't, then it would be after he left her at 7 am. The police doctor was there by 8.45. From her body temperature, he should be able to give us a more accurate time of death.'

'You have a word with him, Hayley. I'll bring the mother in.'

In the lounge, Jack had had his fingerprints taken with the electronic gadget. A swab was taken from his inside cheek for DNA. A police officer was doing the necessaries at the back of the room, out of the way on a small table, inviting them up one at a time, checking them off.

The shock of the death had worn off. No subterfuge now, everyone knew. An hour had passed and Beryl was gone from the world. Jack was sorry she was dead of course, but she'd had no hold on his heart. They had worked together yesterday morning for fifteen minutes, he had enjoyed that. And so had she, delighting in the 3, 4, 5 triangles. There was the kiss at the barbecue. And the invitation to his place, but hardly a meeting of souls.

The meal tonight, with its assorted difficulties, was erased from his timetable. He was free. From a sexual adventure, from work too.

Martin came back into the room.

'How was it?' said Jack.

'They think I did it,' he said. 'The bastards.'

Not inconceivable, thought Jack. When Martin was with his daughter last night he'd have laid mass murder at his doorstep.

'A little early to pin it on you,' he said.

'It's the way they think,' said Martin. 'A young black guy, so must be guilty. All that stop and search; they think we're all carrying guns and knives. I thought they might have changed in the two years I was away, but it's the same, the same. Cops are cops the world over.'

'They haven't charged you?' said Jack.

'A hair's breadth from it.' He indicated the closeness with thumb and finger. 'I wonder where I'll be sleeping tonight. In the tent or in a cell?'

Or with whom, thought Jack. And dismissed the thought as unworthy. A slither of jealousy over a dead woman. He'd never get to heaven. Not with the ape inside him.

'Martin!' called Cleo.

She was in an armchair, and had been half asleep. Up at six, getting ready to feed us lot, thought Jack. She finds the body, shock horror, and now has the repercussions of a murder in her B&B to deal with. And has the best of motives for the deed.

Cleo rose to go to her son, took a couple of steps and then shook, wavered, and collapsed in a heap.

Martin ran to her. 'Mum! What's up, Mum!'

Others crowded round. The police woman from the back of the hall pushed her way through the throng.

'Step aside, please,' she ordered. 'I've had paramedic training.'

Jack had been seated on the arm of a chair, but was now standing with the group watching the young police woman. She was feeling Cleo's pulse, her neck.

'It's not a simple faint,' she said.

Fayyad came into the room.

'What's happened?' he said.

'She's unconscious, sir. We need an ambulance.'

Chapter 24

The police doctor was examining Cleo when the paramedics with the ambulance arrived. She had not recovered consciousness.

'Some sort of poison, I'd guess,' said the doctor, rising, packing away his stethoscope. 'Nothing we can do here.' He turned to the paramedics. 'Get her to hospital without delay. Phone ahead, tell them you are coming, so they'll have a team ready.'

Fayyad and Hayley cleared space around Cleo. The paramedics were quickly in with the stretcher and Cleo placed on it.

'Anyone accompanying her?' asked a paramedic.

'I'll come,' said Martin. 'If it's OK. I'm her son.'

'Fine. Come along.'

They carried her out into the hallway, Martin following, leaving the room subdued. A minute or so later, the siren yowled as the ride began, growing less harsh in the neighbouring streets as the ambulance gathered distance.

'Well, what do you make of that?' said Jean, when the siren had died.

She was seated in an armchair, her black suitcase beside her. She might have been in the business class lounge of an airport.

'Two down,' said George, sitting in the opposite chair.

'She's not dead,' snapped Jack.

'Not yet. But who knows?'

Jack felt like punching him, but indeed, who knows. Something serious. Poison perhaps, the doctor had said. Who? Why? The questions buzzed about his head.

'Jack?' called Fayyad. 'We'll do you now.' And beckoned him to the interview room.

Jack followed Fayyad out, along the corridor and into the TV room. He sat down in the armchair proffered. Hayley was already there.

'I hope Cleo's OK,' he said. 'She just stood up, took a couple of steps, and fell like a bowling pin.'

'The ambulance were quick,' said Hayley. 'They had her on oxygen before they drove off.'

'I'm here to build a base for a summerhouse,' said Jack, wiping his brow with his forearm. 'I never expected this. She was serving breakfast, making coffee. Right as rain. Then she just collapses.' The two women he had his eyes on. He metaphorically slapped his wrist. He was an animal. Despicable. 'I hope it's nothing much,' he said, knowing how feeble that sounded as the words came out.

'Out of our hands,' said Hayley.

Yes, she was. Passed from one set of professionals to another. All the bystanders could do was worry. Never helpful. He took a deep breath and rubbed the back of his neck.

'You OK to begin, Jack?' enquired Fayyad.

'Yeh. Let's go. Nothing else to do.'

Hayley and Fayyad were on the sofa, Hayley with her pen poised, notebook on her lap.

'How well did you know Beryl?' said Fayyad.

'I only met her yesterday. She gave me a hand marking out the site. Seems an age ago. She helped me get the right angles. We flirted last night at the barbecue. She was due to come to my place for dinner tonight...' He threw his hands up. 'And that is my history with Beryl. Oh yes, a kiss on the patio. Nothing more.'

'She was killed between 7.50 and 8.20 this morning,' said Fayyad.

'That precise?'

'The doctor was on the scene within an hour of her death, so a combination of body temperature and blood clotting, according to him, give a narrow window. What were you doing between those times?'

'Right.' He glanced at the clock on the wall. 'Barely two hours ago.' He sucked his lip and thought back. 'I left home at 7.40 on the dot. This place is around five minutes' walk away. So here, say 7.45. And then I worked with Larry for half an hour before breakfast, loading sand, adjusting the planking, for the base I'm making for Cleo's shed. We were called into breakfast at 8.20.'

'Who was present at breakfast?' said Fayyad.

'Everyone but Beryl. Cleo and Martin were serving the food. At the table were me, Jean, Larry, Clyde and what's his name, black slim guy.' He snapped his fingers. 'George.'

'No one flustered or blood stained?'

'Everyone clean and tidy, including me and Larry.'

'Nobody unduly nervous?'

'Not noticeably.'

Fayyad turned to Hayley. 'I think Jack has cut back the window of opportunity by about five minutes...'

'At the very least,' said Hayley. 'The murderer would need to wash off any blood stains and had a weapon to dispose of.'

'Then be at breakfast by 8.20 am. Unflustered.'

'Chop five minutes off, maybe ten,' said Hayley.

'So we are talking about 7.50 to 8.10,' said Fayyad. 'That ties the murder down to a twenty minute gap.'

'You haven't found the weapon?' said Jack.

'No,' said Fayyad. 'We are certainly looking for it.'

'I've lost a club hammer,' he said.

'Ah! Describe it.'

'A small hammer with a squarish, metal head.' He took out his phone, pressed a few buttons. 'Like this.' He showed them a picture.

'Could be the weapon,' said Fayyad looking at the image. 'When did you lose it? Any idea?'

'I was looking for it this morning,' he said. 'Nowhere in the van. And a claw hammer too. You don't need a picture?'

Fayyad smiled. 'I am familiar with claw hammers.'

'I couldn't find them this morning. I think someone took them yesterday while I was working.'

'Who might that have been?'

Jack shrugged. 'Could have been anyone. They were all curious at what we were doing. All of them came over at one time or another. And I could easily have forgotten to pack the hammers away when I left.'

'Not much help.'

Jack shrugged. 'Careless of me.'

'If they turn up, do tell us. Where are we?' He glanced at his notebook. 'Ah yes. What do you know about the relationship between Cleo and Beryl?'

'Well...' he began, reluctant to drop Cleo in it.

'We believe Beryl was blackmailing her,' Fayyad came in helpfully.

'That's what I heard,' he said, 'but I don't know what about.'

'How did you know?'

'Cleo herself told me. She was worried that you'd accuse her of Beryl's murder as she had a clear motive.'

'Do you think she might have done it?'

'No.'

'Her son?'

'I don't know about him. Can't say one way or the other.'

'What about Larry?'

'We were working together all that time. The window, what was it again?'

'Now we are saying, 7.50 to 8.10.'

'Larry and I were working together all that time.'

'How did Larry's wife, Jean, behave? When did she get here? I hear he and his wife are estranged.'

'Jean turned up at the barbecue, and Larry refused to talk to her. Though she kept on trying. Boy, did she try. A most determined woman. She'd booked a room herself but took over Larry's room. He had to sleep in the tent in the garden. This morning, Jean was at breakfast, getting no response from Larry, until his final insult. Now what did he say?' Jack thought back and laughed at the recollection. 'Larry offered her to George. That was it. Way too much for her, and she stormed out, calling us a load of swine.' He shook his head. 'It was a weird breakfast. Only me and Cleo knew Beryl was dead upstairs. The others talking as if she was alive, and noticeable because she wasn't down for breakfast. Jean certainly hated her, that was all too clear. Martin tried to stop her insults, and then others piled in at Jean's expense, leading to her storming out.'

'You say she hated Beryl.'

'Like poison. I got the feeling she was blaming Beryl for turning her husband against her.'

'Plenty to work on there,' said Fayyad. He turned to Hayley. 'Any questions you can think of?'

'One,' she said. She turned to Jack. 'What do you know about George and Clyde?'

'Next to nothing about George, except he says he went to the British Museum yesterday. And Clyde says he was following him. He and Clyde had a fight last night at the barbecue over it. Me and Cleo had to separate them. And oh yes. Clyde isn't Clyde.'

'Who is he then?'

'Don't you recognise him?'

'Should I?' said Fayyad. 'I see a lot of people in this job.'

'Cumberland School. Our year. That help you?'

Fayyad pondered, screwing up his nose.

'I give up. You'd better tell me, Jack.'

'He's Paul Blake.'

'And who is Paul Blake? Sorry, I'm no wiser.'

'Paul Blake was in our year at school. So OK, a lot of classes in our year, and it was more than twenty years ago. But the main point is, he doesn't want to be known. I'd have kept mum but murder is murder, and heaven knows how Cleo is doing.'

'Still can't picture Paul Blake.'

'Football. He and I were in the school team.'

'You know I'm cricket. Strictly cricket. You were the only football player I really knew.'

'He was a defender,' said Jack. 'Pretty good at keeping the goal clear.'

'Excuse me butting in on your school memories,' said Hayley, 'but we're going off piste. We need to know why Clyde changed his name.'

'We do, we certainly do,' said Fayyad. 'Apologies for our nostalgia trip. Let's have Clyde in.' He turned to Jack. 'Thanks for your help.'

'Don't forget the van,' said Hayley.

'Oh yes. Where would I be without you, Hayley? We need to look in your van, Jack. For elimination purposes.'

'Fine.' What else could he say? 'Can I go after you've done the search,' he added.

'I don't see why not.'

Chapter 25

Jack gave the crime-scene manager the keys to his van. He left them to it; there was no point standing over them. Likely, they'd be looking for the murder weapon, blood stained clothing, that sort of stuff. Elimination purposes, wasn't that the wording?

Not likely they'd leave the van untidier than it already was.

Jack joined the others in the lounge just as Hayley came along to collect Clyde for questioning. They left the room together.

'How much longer are they going to keep us?' said Jean to no one in particular, slapping her knees in exasperation, still in her business lounge chair as if she'd booked it, her suitcase by her knees, ready to be checked in. 'I've phoned in to work, told them I'll be in mid afternoon. But the way things are going, today is going to be a write off.'

Larry was reading an old gardening magazine, or appeared to be, engrossed in the possibilities of dahlias and fuchsias. He was seated as far from his wife as possible, working hard to ignore her verbiage.

The CSI woman who had been taking their prints and DNA, having finished, had left. Jack was on the sofa, George by him, stretching his legs, his hands to his chin as if in prayer.

'I wonder what Clyde is telling them,' he said.

'That you followed him,' said Jack.

'That fairy tale! He's paranoid.'

'Why did he pick on you?'

'Because I don't take his nonsense. I stand up for myself. The man drinks like a fish. The only reason he's sober now is that he can't get to his booze. How can he know anything about anyone?'

In the TV room, Clyde was in the armchair, opposite Fayyad and Hayley who were checking notebooks. He was twitching, rubbing his hands together, waiting for the inevitable. Cops were the bane of his life. How much did they know, or would soon find out?

He needed a drink, but couldn't get to his room. He should've left yesterday.

'I'm ready,' he said. 'Can we please begin.'

'We need you to clear up your identity,' said Fayyad, putting down his notebook. 'We know you are, or at least you were, Paul Blake.'

'Did the builder tell you that?'

'No,' Fayyad lied. 'We got it from your fingerprints.'

'Ah,' he said. 'They told me they would destroy them.'

'Overlooked obviously. We have you on record, Clyde. We can look at the circumstances, and we most certainly will. But I'd like to know from you: why have you changed your name?'

Clyde pressed his fists together as he rocked back and forth, resisting what could no longer be resisted.

Fayyad knew he only had to wait. It would come, although he'd half guessed. There weren't many options as Clyde was unlikely to be a gang boss on the run.

'It's all on record,' said Clyde reluctantly. 'But years of holding back, it's hard to break the habit. I don't know how to say it.'

Fayyad interrupted. 'You were on the witness protection programme. Weren't you?'

Clyde smiled with relief. They knew, he didn't have to admit it. They knew.

'I was, I am, I always will be.'

'Tell us how it came about.'

'It's hard to talk about it. Even with you knowing,' said Clyde, looking down at his hands. 'It's shame. Like talking about my sex life to a stranger. But you know, you have it in your records. You're the cops. So here I am. In front of you. Two men at once, that's me. Yes, I was Paul Blake.' He paused, there was no going back. 'I was 23 and working for the Council as a driver,' he went on. 'And I saw a man beaten up and killed by a gang. I was the key witness at the Old Bailey. Four of the gang went down for 20 to 30 years. The Fergusons, you may know of them.'

'I do,' said Hayley. 'Al Ferguson is still around. And up to all sorts of dirty work.'

'Please continue, Clyde.'

'I thought that was it; I'd done my duty as a citizen. I was only 23, what did I know? I was in the hallway of the court, the trial just over, when a cop came up to me. He told me I had to leave the area or I'd be killed. And he would arrange my exit. There was no arguing. He drove me home, and gave me ten minutes to fill a suitcase. I was driven to a house in the countryside. It was the first time I'd heard of the Witness Protection Programme. I was informed I couldn't contact my friends or my family. Three months later, under a different name, with a new passport, a totally different identity, I was put on a flight to Vancouver where I was to set up a new life.' He looked at Fayyad for the first time. 'Paul Blake has been dead for 17 years.'

'So why did you come back, Clyde? You know it's foolhardy.'

'Yes, it's foolhardy. Utterly. Don't I know it. Wasn't it drilled into me, a one way ticket I was given.' He sighed and gazed up at the ceiling. 'I've been married to Susie for thirteen years. We have two girls aged 9 and 11. I'm a realtor, estate agent as they say here. Should be a good life. We have a nice house, girls are doing fine at school.' He brought his head down to face them. 'But secrecy eats into your soul. You can't say a thing to your family, and so, to avoid saying anything, you say less and less about anything at all. I came to doubt who I was. I felt a fraud. I was drinking too much. Warned at work. Susie and I were arguing. Well, hardly me. She was berating me for being uncommunicative. One sided. I was. I am. Who? Who? Do you never wake in the early hours wondering who you are?'

He covered his face with his hands, continuing to talk. 'I never talk like this. Never this many words.' He spoke on, as if his listeners weren't there. 'I needed confirmation.' He slapped his chest. 'To know I have family, not the Vancouver one, but the one that bred me. It wasn't as if I had hated them, left them under a cloud, stolen my mother's savings. Nothing at all like that. I was just gone from their lives, snatched away in the night. From one universe into another. About 18 months ago, in the early hours, when I couldn't sleep, I said to myself I no longer care, I must make contact. And I found online the email address of my sister, Dido. I contacted her. And it went on from there. We emailed, we spoke on Skype. And then a week ago, she told me my mother was dying and she had asked for me. Coincidentally, though I am not sure I believe in coincidence, it was the same day when my wife Susie said she was going to leave me. That was a ball breaker. My pretend life fracturing in front of my eyes. So I flew to England...' He looked up at the pair of them. 'And here I am. Clyde who was Paul.'

'You're risking your life being here, Clyde,' said Fayyad.

'I am beyond caring.'

Fayyad looked at Hayley who was scribbling away. Clyde had stopped his history, as if he were a tyre that had gushed out of air. Exhausted, empty, beyond filling.

'How well did you know Beryl?'

Clyde shrugged. 'The only words I spoke to her was when she told me off for snoring. I do it when I drink, I know. My wife, Susie has me in the spare room. She tells me I sound like a jumbo jet on the runway. But you were asking about Beryl. Nothing to add. Snoring was our only topic.'

'Have you anything to ask, Hayley?'

'No.'

'Thank you, Clyde, for answering our questions. I know it has been difficult. Please go back to the lounge and join the others.'

Clyde rose heavily. He had revealed his life and didn't know where it would lead. Hayley held the door open for him. When he had gone through, she closed it behind him.

'One very depressed man,' she said, sitting on the arm of the sofa.

'It steams off him like water in a sauna.'

'If he stays, they will kill him,' said Hayley. 'Have no doubt. The Fergusons are a nasty bunch. If they get him, or should I say when, they'll cut him into small pieces and feed him to the fishes. Clyde's a dead man, if he doesn't leave town.'

'Will they do it before he tops himself?'

Chapter 26

Jack had gone out to his van. The side door was open with bits and pieces strewn on the pavement. A CSI operative was putting items back.

'Leave it,' said Jack. 'That's if you've finished.'

'All complete,' said the man, togged in white crime scene gear. 'Nothing found.'

'Except my mess,' said Jack. 'I can do some tidying up now.'

'Fine,' said the man. And left him.

Jack looked at the inside of his van and then at the items on the pavement. It always seemed so useless tidying, getting things straight just to make a mess again. There would always be a mess. The mess would win, had to, a law of the universe. Tidiness was unnatural.

He used to tell Alison that he lacked the tidiness gene. Never convincing her, or himself for that matter. It was just the pointlessness of the activity. Sometimes, though, the mess overwhelmed him. So he must do battle against his genes and put things in order. Jack got into the van. First of all, he needed to make more space. He moved a ladder, some buckets he stacked inside each other, a toolbox he put to one side. Various pieces of timber, he laid along the edge and tied them together, so they would stay together. Some of the wood should be thrown away, but you just never knew which piece. The day after you threw it out, you would have to buy the exact same piece.

Or so his excuses went. They lacked logic, even he could see that. Lazy, Alison would say. Mess always wins, he would counter like a teenager justifying his bedroom.

Fifteen minutes of ordering was all he could take. It would have to do. He sat down on the edge of the van, the temperature was on the cool side but he'd warmed up with the work. A stretcher was coming out of the house, carried by two mortuary operatives. A body in transit covered in a sheet, anonymous. The front operative stumbled slightly, and an arm flopped down from under the sheet, white and bloodless. Jack recognised Beryl's purple nail varnish.

Idly, he watched them carry the stretcher along the pavement to their low estate vehicle, the arm swinging as if the stretcher occupant was asleep under the sheet. Two hours ago, someone had hit her on the head. And being methodical, hid the weapon, changed clothes, washed any blood away, and went to breakfast.

He recalled the instant he opened Beryl's door, Cleo behind him, seeing her lying on her back in her short dressing gown, blood seeping into the rug. Time. How it rules us. Half an hour before opening her door, he'd been wrapped in recipes. What to make for dinner this evening. Thinking to impress her with his seeing the holly blue butterfly in the garden. When she was alive and he was making plans for the living woman, with her vibrancy, sexuality.

Plans guillotined in that opened door.

A sharp kick in the soul, a reminder of his mortality. Not an enduring loss, as he had barely known her. But a sadness. For him. A brief grieving for her.

She was a person so little time ago.

The body was slid into the back of the vehicle. And the hinged back slammed down. The two operatives got into the front, and half a minute later were driving away. To the mortuary, he surmised, where there would be an autopsy to add detail on the cause of her death.

By person or persons unknown. One of those at the breakfast table or serving it. The only sure innocent was himself. Of the others, lots of motives. All except Clyde and George, but they couldn't be ruled out. One of them may have interacted with her. Clyde who was really Paul Blake, plenty of mystery there.

A curious job his friend Fayyad had. Homing in on the most guilty in a group. Though he was doing it himself. Couldn't help it.

Maybe that was a gene he had. The curiosity one, the fitting together one. It had eliminated the tidiness gene. As if genes were fighting fish.

Then there was Cleo and her mysterious collapse. What was that all about? Martin had gone with his mother to the hospital. It could be nothing much, or it could be deadly serious. Another murder, or what?

What a morning!

It surprised him how he was more involved with Cleo. Not simply because she was alive. Beryl was forever temporary. She had slept around, his liaison with her would have been short. She would have moved on quickly. A holly blue after a new bloom. Or he might have found her too high maintenance to justify the sex.

Cleo was different. It was he that she had come for when she'd found the body. That moment of trust. Not altogether kosher, as he recalled calculating if sleeping with Beryl would spoil his chances with Cleo. Sex stomped all over it.

Clyde came out of the house, in his grey suit, wearing a trilby hat. He was pushing a suitcase on wheels. Jack rose and dizziness rocked him. He put a hand on the van to steady himself, his head whirring.

'Are you alright?' said Clyde, stopping a few yards away.

'I've come over dizzy,' he said. He was shaky on his feet, the world a little blurry. 'It's nothing much. Be OK in a sec.'

'Diabetes?' queried Clyde.

'Yes,' said Jack. He lowered himself slowly down to the edge of the van, sitting, feet pressing the ground, waves of dizziness washing through him. 'I had a light breakfast at home, meant to eat here but with the murder and everything...'

Clyde was sorting through his jacket pocket. He brought out a tube of sweets.

'I have diabetes too, one of the ten percent,' he said. 'I always keep emergency glucose just in case. You should too. Here, take a couple.'

He passed a couple of wrapped lozenges. Jack took them gratefully. Unwrapping one, he placed it in his mouth. It was cold, powdery and sweet on his tongue.

'Don't swallow it. Smooth it into your tongue,' said Clyde. 'Use your finger. That way it goes straight into the bloodstream.'

Jack did as he was bid and rubbed in the powdery sweetness. Then did the same with the other lozenge. Recovery was coming, the dizziness waning.

'It's a temporary remedy,' said Clyde. 'Now you must eat something substantial.'

'I've sandwiches in the van,' said Jack. He eased himself up, yes, he was feeling better. 'Where you off to?'

'I'm going to Newham Hospital.'

'I could drive you,' said Jack. 'I want to find out about Cleo, anyway.'

'A lift would be fine,' said Clyde. 'But I think I should drive.'

Chapter 27

Clyde drove. They stopped at Jack's flat just up the road, Clyde stayed in the van, and Jack went in and took his medicine with a little water, and was back out in a few minutes. They headed south, down Upton Lane, Jack munching a sandwich he'd made in the morning for lunch.

'No satnav,' said Clyde.

'I work mostly locally,' said Jack as he ate, feeling better. 'Don't need it.'

'Let's see if I can still remember the way. More fun than satnav.'

'You drive the van well.'

'We have one at work that I drive sometimes. Has power steering and satnav though.'

'Our American cousin boasting.'

'Canadian,' said Clyde sharply. 'And you're right. Why should I knock your van? It serves you well enough. It's obvious you're not rich.'

'Nor likely to be,' said Jack, 'short of winning the lottery.'

'And where would I be without builders? We're parasites you know, us realtors. We live off house owners and builders.'

'You tell lies, if you don't mind me saying.'

'We exaggerate, let's say. But you needn't worry, the internet is replacing us with seller to seller sales. I wonder what jobs will be left when everything's done online. What will people do for a living?'

'It'll be like the 19th century,' said Jack, 'with the poor queuing cap in hand to be servants for the rich.'

'A bleak picture. Now, this must be Green Street. Yes, all the sari shops and jewellers. I came down it on the bus yesterday. Like little Bombay.'

'How can there be so many sari shops?'

'They don't buy them online, Jack. They like the social side of shopping. That's what I always say to justify my job. Interaction, person to person, eye contact, customer service. You know, I haven't talked this much in ages. The cops got me talking. I couldn't stop rabbiting.'

'About who you really are?'

'Yes. All that. But you recognised me. I'll deny it no longer. I was at Cumberland. Paul Blake, that was me.'

'So why aren't you Paul Blake now?'

'The big question. Why does a man deny his identity. Have a guess.'

'Someone's after you.'

'Spot on. I'm in the witness protection programme. I saw a man killed and was the key witness at the trial. So they shipped me off to Canada, name change and all. Please don't say a word of this to anyone.'

'How could I?' said Jack. 'A fellow footballer. We were in the Cumberland school team. Like the Freemasons. On my Cumberland football oath, I shall stay shtum. You were a good defender.'

'We won the Newham School Championship in my last year.'

'The only reason I attended school, to keep in the team. Skipped half the lessons, which is why I'm so dumb.'

'You're not dumb at all. Just missed out on some schooling. Not the same thing. What's happened to West Ham Stadium? Should be just here.'

'West Ham have moved to the 2012 Olympic Stadium. Now called the London Stadium.'

'That's going up in the world. How the Hammers doing?'

'So so.' Jack shrugged. 'Evading relegation each year, just about. Getting through managers like pies on match day.'

'Right. Let's stop.' Clyde pulled into the side of the road. 'There's a pharmacy. You want glucose tablets. Not sweets, but compressed powder that breaks up in your mouth. Gives quick relief.'

'You sound like a TV ad.'

'I'm a realtor. I know how to market a product. Except when it comes to myself. Jump out.'

Jack left Clyde at the wheel and dived into the shop. He told the Asian woman at the counter what Clyde had told him. And she went straight for it and held out a box of twelve lozenges.

'You diabetic?' she said as she handed over the box.

'Yes.'

'Only use them in an emergency,' she said. 'You must not develop a taste for them. They're not sweets. Your body is bad at handling sugars: glucose, sucrose and fructose. Take your medication regularly and you shouldn't need these.'

'You're doing yourself out of business,' he said.

She smiled broadly. 'I don't want you to die.'

'That makes two of us.'

He thanked her, recalling Doctor Aziz telling him that diabetes was high in the Asian community. Likely, she had plenty of customers like him. It was a new world, so many seduced by junk food. Almost a community in itself.

Jack left the shop and returned to the van where Clyde was speaking out of the window to a black traffic warden. The van was on a double yellow line, which would be 80 quid.

But the traffic warden was smiling and nodding.

'Let's go before he changes his mind,' said Clyde aside.

He put the van into gear and drove off, giving a brief wave to the warden who waved back.

'His parents were from Kingston,' said Clyde, 'so I said so were mine.'

'And they weren't?'

'Another exaggeration. Barbados actually, a thousand miles south west. Still Caribbean though, so that counts. And they went to Kingston on their way to the UK.'

'That's the World Cup statue,' pointed out Jack. 'See, three West Ham players in the 1966 England team. From a photo of the time. Bobby Moore on their shoulders holding the Jules Rimet cup.'

'Bobby Moore's dead.' Adding after a second, 'Lucky man.'

'Why do you say that?'

'The benefits of living are exaggerated. Moore won the World Cup. I haven't. And never will. Though I did play football in Vancouver for a couple of years. I shouldn't have said that. Not where I've been living. I'm talking too much. Those cops. Got me spieling like a tap that won't turn off. What does it matter, I'm a nowhere man. I should stand on a soapbox and tell everyone, here I am, Paul Blake. Come and get me. Down here for the hospital.' He turned left at the traffic lights. 'You know the worst feeling ever?'

'What's the worst feeling?'

'Up and over the Sewerbank.' He was looking at the low rise ahead.

'Called Greenway now.'

'A marketing man's make-over. Must have been an estate agent. What was I saying? I'm all over the place. My wife is leaving me. I've never talked this much to her, not real talk. Where was I? Ah yes, the worst feeling. Take it from one who knows. It is emptiness. When you feel you are nothing, have no place in the world. A psychological refugee.' He waved a dismissive hand. 'It's not self pity. I am beyond that. It's simply I am lost. No satnav or map and all the street names are in Japanese.'

'You could ask someone.'

Clyde gave a short laugh. 'You have to know where you want to go to do that.'

They had turned into the short road that led to the hospital. And up the slight rise, driving slowly along the length of Newham University Hospital, often called by its old name Newham General. Or just Newham. The architecture was boxy, undistinguished, opened by the Queen in 1983, and the university section by Diana, Princess of Wales, a few years later.

They pulled into the car park, where Clyde had no difficulty parking as this wasn't a busy time. He turned off the engine.

'Coming over on the plane, I hardly knew why I was going, except my wife said she was leaving me, so why not? My mother was dying. Did I really need to see her after seventeen years away? She would die with or without me. That's callous, but I have been thinking a lot about death. On the flight, I thought how I might kill myself. Drive over a cliff. Though you might survive the drop and be in a wheelchair the rest of your life. Step in front of a bus. The bus might be going too slow. I figured the best way is to jump from a high building. Tenth floor say. A leap out into the blue. You know how long it takes to fall a hundred feet?'

'No.'

'Two and a half seconds. Hardly time for your life to flash before you. It's: one elephant, two elephants, three ele...' He snapped his fingers. 'And you hit the ground at 66 miles per hour. Your bones blast into your heart, lungs and guts like bullets. Your backbone will shoot out of your head, before the bones break in turn. You are gone, smashed up, done with. No thought or feeling left, no need for glucose tablets, just a mash of flesh and bone on the pavement.'

'Pity the people who have to scrape you up.'

'But I am gone. Over with. I leave pity to those alive, enjoying life.' He gave a half laugh as if he'd been telling a joke. 'Take no notice of me. I get like this. My wife calls me misery guts. I don't know what world I am in. They say you should be grateful for life. Thank God for it. I can't, I'm afraid.' He turned to Jack. 'Thank you for the lift here. I'm going up to see my mother. I went yesterday, she didn't know me. All pointless really. You must go to reception to find out where Cleo is. I hope she's OK.'

He put out his hand. Jack shook it.

'Look after yourself,' he said.

And tried to think of something more inspiring as Clyde climbed out of the van. He got as far as thinking about the old football team, the school, but Clyde was walking away. You have forgotten your suitcase, he was about to call after him, but hesitated, and then Clyde was too far off to hear.

He had the uncomfortable feeling that Clyde had left it behind on purpose.

Chapter 28

Jack asked at reception for the whereabouts of Cleo Dickens who had been brought in earlier by ambulance. He was told Canning Ward on the top floor. Jack took the stairs rather than the lift, which he always did for short climbs. And wondered, as he was climbing, should he have? Why take chances? But he couldn't treat himself like an invalid, not if he intended to keep on working. Besides, he'd eaten and taken his medication.

He had to take control. Learn about this new condition and how to pace himself. What to eat and not eat. He had glucose tablets for emergency, Clyde's advice. And thinking about it, he should keep his medication with him. Set the times to take it on his phone.

Be organised. Treat it like work.

On the top floor, he followed the directions for the ward, as he walked up the long corridor which traversed the length of the hospital. On each side were the doors to wards for every condition affecting the human body. Not quite all: he thought of Clyde's death wish. It's everyone's right to kill themselves, but, but, but... It's an awful final choice. A failure of community. We should...

Should, that untidy word. We should, he should, it should. Change your life or jump out of a window. How could he decide for Clyde, who was torn away from friends and family for being a good citizen seventeen years ago. Jack might say he would not act that way himself, but how did he know? He had never been there.

Not quite true. When he'd been drinking, that was a daily suicide, a desire to kill yourself for the time being. Advice was easy to give. Cheap. Like quack medicine on a spoon. It often left a nasty taste and didn't work.

On either side, as he strolled the corridor, the ill, the very ill, the dying. He hated hospitals. Been in too many in his drunken days, picked up off the streets, carted in by ambulance, told by doctors that he was killing himself. Wasting resources. The message had seeped into his half pickled brain eventually, and Jack had gone to Alcohol Halt. Where they said the same thing, more or less. Life will be worth living when you give up alcohol.

One bit of sound advice amongst the dross. Beware of whom you listen to.

There it was: Canning Ward. Jack pushed open the double doors. Just ahead was the nurses' station. He asked a woman in nurse uniform where he might find Cleo Dickens.

'Room G,' she pointed out. 'She's very ill.'

At least she was alive. He thanked her, and headed down the corridor. On either side were open side wards with four to six beds in. He came to Room G and looked through the glass window in the door. There was Martin, seated by the only bed, with Cleo almost hidden in monitors, wires and tubes.

He went in.

Martin lit up to see Jack, and rose to greet him.

'Hiya, Jack. Good to see you.' They shook hands at the foot of the bed. 'She's in a bad way, hasn't regained consciousness.'

'She looks awful.'

Cleo was pale, almost blue, breathing imperceptibly. A drip was going into her arm. Wires were going from her head and body to the various monitors registering the life in her, illustrated in pulsating waves and numbers.

'She's going for an operation in half an hour. Her liver, something like that. I only took in half of what the doctor said.'

'Do you want something to eat?'

'I haven't any money.'

'I'll get it. There's nothing we can do here.'

They left unconscious Cleo.

At her bed and breakfast, Earlham Lodge, Larry was being questioned by Hayley and Fayyad, seated in the customary armchair and they on the sofa. Hayley had her notebook open and was taking notes.

'You slept in the tent in the garden last night,' said Fayyad. 'Why was that?'

Larry was in the grubby t-shirt that he'd changed into earlier and the trousers still on from the barbecue. He had a mug of tea, that had been supplied by a police constable, as they'd been in the lounge several hours awaiting interview.

'I had no choice but sleep in the tent,' he said. 'My wife, Jean, had taken over my room and wasn't going to leave.'

'Why was that?'

'I had emailed her that I wasn't coming back. Somewhat rude, but I wasn't feeling polite. Our marriage has failed. And really I have to look after myself. But she caught the train down and was demanding answers to I hardly know what question.'

'You told her that you were having an affair. Have you been?'

'Is that what Jean told you?'

'She did. For two months, she said.'

'Well, I haven't been. It's a lie I told her, so she'd think the worst of me and leave me alone. Except it didn't work. She came down anyway and demanded an explanation. Took over my room, so I slept in the tent.'

'You have pretended to be working the last couple of months.'

'Oh dear, everything's coming out. My life. It couldn't go on, I suppose. I'm an awful coward. I was sacked. Leave the premises, don't come back, they said.'

'Why were you sacked?'

'Do I have to say? Is it relevant?'

'We could phone your office and find out from them.'

'And I'm sure you would. Oh dear, no secrets allowed. You are nosy. Delving into everything.'

'It's our job,' said Fayyad. 'I doubt you'll shock us with your answer. Why were you sacked, Larry?'

'Porn and call girls on my computer. Human Resources flagged it up. I had no excuses, it was true. No sex with my wife for years now.' He sighed. 'This is such a miserable tale. Like many lonely men, I bought sex and looked at pictures of men screwing. Very juvenile. Quite pathetic. On my work computer. Dumb on dumb.' He held out his helpless hands. 'So they had me in, and I was out. Silly, wretched, piteous. I couldn't leave work quick enough. And from then on, I pretended to be working, like grown-ups do.' He shrugged. 'It was bound to catch up with me, but you go on day by day, and hope you can get by for another one.'

Fayyad glanced at his notebook.

'As you slept in the tent, Larry, where was the intended occupant?'

'Martin, you mean. He was upstairs in Beryl's room. Poor Babs. Did he kill her?'

'He is a suspect. But then everyone is. Including yourself.'

'I gathered that. But I didn't do it. I get on well...' He stopped himself and shrugged. 'Got on well with my sister. Too well for Jean, who hated her for it. I baby sat for Babs as a child. I'm ten years older. The name Babs dates from then. We collected butterflies together. We go...' He put up a hand to stop himself. 'Went to the theatre some evenings. It's awful. Awful. I am bereft.'

156

'Who will inherit her estate?'

'I haven't seen the will. Is there one? Don't know. I would think I'd get some of it.'

'Maybe all of it?'

'I don't know. I don't want to think about it. I am cut in half, my sister gone. We looked after each other. Me when she was divorcing, she now I'm unemployed.'

'We've been looking through the accounts of the B&B,' said Fayyad. 'You're on a cheap rate, Larry. Why is that?'

'Beryl negotiated that.'

'From what we can see, she didn't seem to be paying anything.'

'I think she did the audit for Cleo. Some deal?' He shrugged. 'Maybe she pays in arrears. I've never discussed it with her.' His hands went to his cheeks in panic. 'I was about to say you'll have to ask her. How can someone be rubbed out, just like that? Gone from the world. In perfect health, she was about to become a partner in her firm.'

Fayyad looked to Hayley. She nodded.

'What were you doing between 7.50 and 8.10 this morning?' he said.

'Is that when she was killed?'

'Just answer the question, please.'

'I was working, all the time, with Jack. He's my witness. He was bringing in the sand, I was raking it flat. On the site. It's to be the base for Cleo's shed. Summerhouse, she calls it. How is she? Do you know?'

'Very ill. That's from about an hour ago. I can't give you an update.'

'What a house! First one thing then another.'

Fayyad looked to Hayley. 'Any questions?' She shook her head. 'That'll do for now, Larry. But I'd like you to go to the police station tomorrow morning. Let's say 10 am. And we'll do a full taped interview. It's for your protection, rather than our scribbled notes.'

Chapter 29

Jack and Martin were in the hospital café, fairly full as it was lunchtime but they'd managed to get a small table to themselves. Clyde was there too, talking earnestly to a black woman about his age. From her similar features, Jack presumed she was his sister.

Martin had fish and chips with a side salad. Jack looked at it enviously. Chips were to be occasional for him, fish yes but not fried. He had a salad, as he'd eaten his sandwiches in the van on the way to the hospital. They both had a mug of tea.

'I don't like salad,' said Jack, picking at it with his fork. 'It just isn't substantial. So little taste to these green leaves. You have to smother them in mayonnaise.'

'So why'd you get it?'

'Doctor's orders. Cut back on junk food. Which means anything fried is out. What's yours like?'

'The fish is bland, just filler. They know how to cook fish in Venezuela. I worked on a street stall for a couple of months, selling fried fish. This is battered to death; I've no idea what it was alive. If it ever was. The chips are fine. I'm OK on salad.' He stopped his dietary ramble. 'Got something for you.' He took out a piece of scrunched up paper from his pocket, and handed it to Jack.

It was so screwed up, the writing faint, that Jack could barely read it. Then it hit him.

'That's my daughter's phone number,' he said. 'How'd you get that?'

'She left it in my tent.' He forked a couple of chips and ate them, casually as if such things happened all the time. 'Tear it up.'

Jack was angry, working hard to keep his temper.

'How do I know you don't have it on your phone?' he said.

'I don't have a phone.'

Jack stuffed the paper in his pocket and sipped tea. His mind was blazing.

'Were you going to sleep with her?'

'I didn't know her age. Mum told me.'

'Were you going to ask?'

'Yes.'

Jack didn't believe him. wrath welling. He couldn't have a row here, with all these people. And Martin had come clean. He needn't have done. Jack worked to quell his fury.

'It's not the same in Venezuela,' said Martin with a shrug. 'Age is not an issue.'

Jack had no idea whether that was true or not.

He said, 'You can get five years for sleeping with a minor.'

'No thanks.'

He's a good looking fellow, thought Jack, so why? Like a young Jimi Hendrix, hair like a tree blown in the wind.

'It's flying in,' said Martin. 'I was jet lagged, been away two years. Didn't think about it.'

'There must be some way outta here, said the joker to the thief,' recited Jack.

'Dylan, but I prefer the Hendrix version,' said Martin. A chip to his mouth, adding, 'Who's the joker, who's the thief?'

Jack didn't comment, thinking Martin could play both parts. For distraction, he tried some tomato and lettuce. It was as insipid as he'd expected but something to chew, other than speak in a temper.

'My mum likes you,' said Martin.

'I like her.'

He wondered if that was why Martin had given him the phone number. He didn't have to. A peace offering.

'I can see you're angry,' said Martin. He'd pushed the remnant of fish aside and was working on the chips.

'Wouldn't you be?'

'Probably. But I keep my nest clean, as they say. My mum likes you, you bought me lunch, I'm not going to cause you trouble.'

He had a broad, winning smile.

'I hope you're genuine,' said Jack.

'I play for the team.'

'We're a team now?'

'You're working for my mum, you came to see her in hospital, you bought me lunch...'

Jack held up a hand to stop him.

'Enough, enough. Don't give me a halo. All right, I'm worried about Cleo. Who wouldn't be? And anyone half decent would have bought you a meal.'

'Plenty wouldn't.'

'Maybe I wanted to sound you out.'

'Said the joker to the thief.'

'Just stay away from Mia. Understand me?'

'Clear, way too clear. I'm drowning in the message. You'll get no trouble from me, Jack. On my mother's life. Hell. Shouldn't say that. Not here, now. Bad luck, you know, in Venezuela. Lots of voodoo. I didn't think. She's going into theatre...'

'I take your promise. And you take mine. So let's get off the subject of my daughter.'

They ate in silence. Jack had no way of proving the sincerity of Martin, though his little outburst for his mother half convinced him. And he knew Jimi Hendrix. Can't be all bad. He would have to talk to Mia. Not a comfortable conversation. Fourteen year olds! The quicker she grew up the better.

'They think I did it, you know,' said Martin. 'The cops. They were laying it on me so hard.' He did an imitation of a New York cop. 'You were the last one to see her alive, buster, you had de time and de motive.' He laughed at his attempt. 'They could've said, you're young and black, that's enough for any hung jury. I get so mad.'

'They have to prove it.'

'They could fit me up easy enough.'

'I know Fayyad, the Asian cop. He wouldn't do that.'

Martin screwed his lips. 'I don't trust cops. Any of them. They team up to get you. Plant evidence, lie.'

'You've been in prison, haven't you?'

'Yeh. A year for drugs. Young offenders institution, Feltham.'

'Did they fit you up?'

'Yeh. They sure did.' He paused, the sign of a story he'd told before. 'They said it was half a kilo when it was a kilo. I wonder where the other half went.' He laughed. 'I was walking down the street. King of East Ham. I wouldn't say I was minding my own business because I had a delivery to make. They stopped me looking for weapons. Instead they found snow. When I came out a year had gone by. And they kept stopping me, searching me, telling me they'd get me sooner or later. It's why I went abroad.'

'And changed your ways.'

'Not entirely.' He laughed, leaving Jack to wonder what dirty games he'd been involved in.

Martin was a charmer. And winning over Jack. He hoped he wasn't being soft soaped.

Jack had forgotten about Clyde. But movement at the table drew him. The woman was leaving him. Clyde waved to her, she back, and she left the café. Once she'd gone, he looked around him. Jack took care not to catch his eye.

161

Clyde took out a small bottle of spirits and poured a heavy slug into a coffee cup. He put the bottle away and drank from the cup.

Jack knew what was going on. Clyde hadn't wanted to drink in front of his sister but was making up for it now. That was quite a draught in the cup.

'He drinks too much,' said Martin, seeing where Jack was looking. 'He's got some trouble. I don't know what, but he's in a fix.'

'He is,' mused Jack. Identity trouble, drink and a failed marriage. Jack had been too far up the same road.

Clyde rose, pushed his chair in and walked, staggering a little, out of the cafe.

'I'm going to follow him,' said Jack.

'Why?'

'I'm worried about him.'

He rose and set off. Martin caught him up as he was coming out of the café door.

'I'll come. Nothing to do here. Come back later. And there's just cops at the B&B.'

'Don't cause me any trouble.'

'We're a team.'

Jack smiled, not convinced by the truth of it, but the smile was warm.

Clyde was easy to follow. He walked slowly, so they were able to stay well back. He didn't look round as he left the hospital and came out into the car park. And there, getting out of a car, was George. Smart casual, the apparent tourist. Though a local hospital didn't usually feature on a tripper's bucket list.

Jack held Martin back at the entrance.

'Stay a mo'. See George there? Clyde says he's been following him. Let's see if it's so.'

George paid the driver. Must be a taxi. Jack wondered how long he'd been waiting in the vehicle for Clyde to emerge. A well paid gig, obviously. George stepped behind a car where Jack couldn't see him. The taxi driver got back into his vehicle and drove off. And there was George again, hanging back, behind a car, not wishing to be seen by Clyde who was leaving the car park. He turned on to the pavement and was heading along the length of the hospital to the main road.

George came out from behind the car, walking rapidly to lessen the distance between him and Clyde, then slowed to Clyde's pace.

'He's tailing him all right,' said Martin. 'No doubt about that.'

'Why do you think he'd do that?'

'Must be a private eye or a hit man.' He gave a half smile as if sharing a secret with Jack. 'Or both.'

'My thinking too. Let's find out which. We'll follow George.'

They let him get about 50 yards ahead, and trailed him.

Chapter 30

In the lounge of the B&B Fayyad and Hayley were drinking coffee. They had completed the interviews, and allowed the residents to leave if they wished. All had vacated the premises after the stress of the event, and their interviews.

'So what do you think?' said Fayyad. He was looking at his notebook, turning the pages for a hint, for an association, for something unexplained.

'Could be Martin,' she said thoughtfully. 'I'm sure he could do it. Could be his mother. Could be Martin and Cleo in cahoots. That'd make an interesting trial. Each blaming the other in the dock. That would excite the tabloids. Or could be Jean. Classic sister-in-law jealousy. Could be Larry but he was working with Jack. And I can't see why it would be Jack. Though George bothers me.'

'Why?'

'Too smooth. Says he's a private eye. Well, some of them are pretty dubious. Just a cover to do dirty tricks. Says he's on holiday.'

'And Clyde says George has been following him.'

'Clyde drinks and has a suspicious nature for obvious reasons. Which is not to say George isn't following him. Or maybe George being here has something to do with Beryl. She was blackmailing Cleo, maybe others. Auditors get around, sexually she gets around. The only one I'm inclined to rule out is Clyde. But then maybe I shouldn't be ruling him out because I am ruling him out.'

She laughed.

'And Jack,' said Fayyad, 'have you let him off too easily?'

'He's your pal, isn't he?'

'He is.'

'That puts him well in the frame.'

Fayyad laughed. 'I'd give you a hundred to one it isn't Jack.'

'The trouble with our job,' she said, 'is that you don't trust anyone.'

'Not even your own mother,' said Fayyad.

'She's clean,' said Hayley.

The CSI manager came in. He was in white cover-gear from head to foot, but had drawn back the hood, and the mask was round his neck.

'Hi, guys. I've something for you.'

'What's that, Steve?'

Steve held up two transparent evidence bags, one in each hand. In each was a small brown bottle.

'This stuff,' he said. 'It's a poison. I've come across it before. I was attached to Foreign Crime for a couple of years.' He held one of the bags up. 'This one labelled A is the poison. The Russians perfected it. A few drops is enough for anyone. The victim will die in 12 hours without the antidote.' He held up the other bag. 'This one, labelled B, is the antidote. Give it in time and you'll get a full recovery. It's a great system. You poison the victim, and then send them home. Either the relatives pay the ransom and the victim gets the antidote. Or he or she will die.'

'Nasty stuff,' said Hayley.

'You then have a dead man walking around the house, phoning his bank, pleading for his life from his relatives. The clock ticking.'

Hayley shuddered.

'I shouldn't be surprised at any way of killing,' she said, 'but this one does it. So cold and clever.'

'Where did you find them?' said Fayyad.

'The bottle of poison was found in the room where Cleo slept last night. The antidote in George's room. The thing is, the poison bottle top was loose, and leaky. I reckon Cleo got some on her fingers. And probably licked them.'

'And that would be enough?' said Hayley.

'It's deadly stuff. Just takes a few drops to fell a horse.'

'We have to get the antidote to the hospital,' said Fayyad rising from the chair. 'Straight away.'

'Full blues and twos,' said Hayley, getting up.

In less than a minute, they were off, blue light flashing and the two tone siren wailing. Hayley drove while Fayyad phoned the hospital, telling them they were coming with the antidote for Cleo Dickens.

Chapter 31

Jack and Martin were tailing George, and trying to look inconspicuous. It was difficult with the slow pace of Clyde, who was dictating the pace of his shadows. He was walking up Green Street, past what had been West Ham football stadium, now luxury flats. A leisurely stroll, as Clyde kept stopping, at a wall, at a street light to support himself, with George, Martin and Jack having to find reasons to halt. Shop windows, bus stops, once to admire a hedge in flower though Jack had not the slightest idea what it was.

It had no perfume, and lots of tiny florets. A striped bee was hopping to and fro. That'd be a cunning way to follow someone, an artificial bee. Weren't male bees called drones, he recalled from somewhere. And Clyde was off again.

A little further on, Clyde sat on a wall and finished off his bottle. And then he kept it with him until he found a bin to dump it in. Jack was surprised at the tidiness of the semi drunk, a group not known for such habits, but maybe it was the realtor in him overruling the boozer this once.

They passed Queen's Market, busy and darkish under its roof. A smell of spices wafted out from the myriad food stalls. The closest stall had a group of Asian women around rolls of multi-coloured cloth. A little beyond, hands of plantain were hanging from hooks over a stall where deep brown yams had been made into a tower of rough logs.

Up ahead, George had turned into Upton Park station after Clyde.

'Quick,' exclaimed Jack. 'The two of them will be catching the tube.'

He and Martin ran to the station. As they came to the entrance, travellers poured out. A train had obviously just come in.

In the foyer, Jack leaned against the wall to keep out of the mêlée. In his wallet, he sorted out his Oyster card, the permanent ticket for use on the tube. By the time he'd found it, he'd lost sight of Martin.

And then spotted him, the other side of the turnstile, beckoning Jack. He must have tail-gated his way through, close behind a ticket holder. A minor offence, way down from underage sex.

Jack went through and joined him.

'Took your time,' said Martin.

'I'm a law abiding citizen,' said Jack. 'Most of the time.'

Ahead of them were the stairs to the platform for trains going into London. Along the corridor were the stairs to trains heading the other way, out to Barking and Upminster.

'Which way did they go?' said Jack.

'Don't know.'

'I'll go straight down, you take the other, Jimi boy. Quick, before a train gets in.'

Jack set off down the stairs. Upton Park station was busy, even early afternoon, the quickest way in or out of town from these parts.

Once on the platform, he gazed along the length, having to move back and forth, trying to spot Clyde amongst all the people. There were recesses, here and there, so Jack had to walk further down to make sure he wasn't in any of them or at the far end. A train was coming in on this platform.

He wasn't here, Jack was pretty sure. So Clyde must be on the other. Jack ran back along the platform to the steps, and swiftly up them, to beat the passengers getting off the train. Only thinking at the top of the stairs that perhaps he shouldn't be running. But he carried on anyway, along the corridor, and jumped down the steps to the other platform.

At the bottom was Martin. He was holding a wallet and phone, looking into the compartments of the wallet.

'Where'd you get those?' said Jack.

'From George.'

'How the hell...' And stopped himself, a pointless question. 'Don't tell me. Something you learned in Venezuela. Along with frying fish and voodoo.'

'Had to make a living somehow.'

Jack didn't bother to answer.

'Where are they?'

Eyes peeled, he was heading down the platform, Martin following. And he spotted Clyde, about halfway down, standing too close to the edge, easily visible between other travellers.

'He's going to jump,' exclaimed Jack. 'I know it.'

'There's a train coming,' pointed out Martin. A hundred yards off, a tube was hammering in.

Jack raced down the platform, edging in between people to get to Clyde. This was what he had dreaded, he had sensed it, an end of life weariness in Clyde. Not belonging anywhere, the desire to leave the world, once and for all.

An Asian man in traditional whites stepped in front of Jack, who couldn't halt in time. They collided, the man falling to the ground.

Jack stopped for half a second.

'Sorry, sorry,' he declared, 'someone I've got to help. Sorry.'

'Be more careful. Don't rush,' said the man in annoyance to Jack's back.

The tube train was coming in, slowing, perhaps fifty yards off. There was Clyde, so close to the edge, as if on a diving board about to demonstrate a double somersault in the piked position.

He had to get to him before the train.

Jack sprinted. And was there, breathless. He jerked at Clyde's arm, pulling him back. Just as George came in with both hands to push Clyde. But Clyde was no longer there. Just air. No barrier to his impetus.

George was flailing, arms wheeling, stumbling. Unable to halt himself, he was over the platform edge, in mid air as the train struck him.

A second of silence as the train glided on, then screaming, and yelling in English and a variety of languages.

'There's a man under the train!'

'I don't believe what I just saw.'

'Did you see him jump!'

'That poor driver!'

Excitement and shock traversed the platform. A death in front of them, that some had seen and some had missed. An adrenaline flood as strangers declared, gesticulated, pointed out where it had happened, attempting to explain what they had witnessed in a fleeting instant.

The train had stopped, the front of it at the end of the platform. Jack drew Clyde back from the platform edge.

'Were you going to jump?' said Jack.

They were well back, although there was no danger. Clyde was shaky as if he hardly knew where he was.

'I was looking at the lines, thinking of cold steel and electricity,' he said. 'I might have jumped. But it was too quick. Someone fell, I think. Did they fall? Or maybe it was me.'

He was tottering, his legs having trouble holding him upright. Jack settled him against a wall where he slid to the ground. Martin joined them. An announcement came over the tannoy in an Asian accent.

'The train on Platform 1 will not be going any further. There has been an incident. Please alight and make your journey by other means. Passengers, do not get on the train. I repeat, do not get on the train. It will not be going anywhere. There has been an accident.'

Bewildered passengers were getting off, asking one another what was going on. Why was their train not proceeding with its journey?

The announcement was repeated.

Jack said to Clyde, 'Give me your wallet.'

'It's mine. You can't have it.' Clyde was befuddled.

'Don't argue. Give me it.'

When he plainly was not going to give it up, Jack went for Clyde's pocket and pulled it out. Clyde was beyond resistance and settled back against the wall, head nodding, eyes blinking. Jack looked in the wallet. There was some money in notes and a bus photo card for Clyde Rogers.

'That'll do.'

Jack stepped between the alighting passengers and dashed to where George had fallen. Along the platform, station staff were ushering passengers up the stairs and away from the stationary train. Jack dropped down as if to do up a shoelace. Surreptitiously, he edged the wallet between the train and platform. It fell onto the line.

He stood up and returned to the others.

'I hope that wasn't seen,' he said.

'I never saw,' said Martin. 'What did you do?'

'If you didn't see then probably no one else did.'

'I don't understand.'

'Clyde Rogers is dead,' he said. 'He fell under a tube train at Upton Park. Let's get out of here.'

Chapter 32

They attempted to walk back to the hospital where Jack had left his van. Clyde was drunk, no longer any uncertainty in his condition, the alcohol soaked into his brain. He was staggering, every so often resting on a wall, or gripping a lamppost like a long lost friend.

'We'll be here all year at this rate,' said Jack.

He spotted a black cab and hailed it. The cab pulled to a halt by the side of the road, a little way up.

'I hope I've enough cash,' he said.

'George will pay,' said Martin, waving the wallet that he'd purloined.

'Well, he won't need it now.'

Jack told the driver their destination was the hospital. The driver looked dubiously at Clyde.

'He's a diabetic,' said Jack. 'Groggy. Likely to go into a coma.'

'We'd better get him to the hospital quick,' said the cabbie. 'Jump in.'

They climbed in the taxi. It took the efforts of both Jack and Martin to get Clyde in the seat. The driver looked back to make sure they were all belted up. And set off.

'I'm still thinking it out,' said Martin. 'What you did back there. You dropped Clyde's wallet on the line.'

'I did. And you stole George's wallet and phone,' said Jack, 'so the only ID they'll find with the body is Clyde's. So they'll assume, naturally enough, that body is Clyde. It will be so mashed up, as to be unidentifiable.'

'One black man looks much like another,' said Martin.

'Even more so, if he's been under a train.'

'Good thinking, Batman,' mused Martin. 'And it means I've got some time with this little bundle.' He was going through George's wallet. 'There's well over a hundred quid here. And bingo! A contactless credit card.'

'Be careful with it,' said Jack.

'No one will know that he's dead for ages. You saw to that. Maybe never.' He waved the card. 'This is my meal ticket. I hope he has plenty in the account.'

In five minutes, they were at the hospital where they alighted. Martin paid the cab fare in cash.

'I'm going off to see how mum is,' he said.

'I'm going to take Clyde to Heathrow,' said Jack. 'That's if he has his flight ticket with him. He left his suitcase in my van, so I'm hoping it's in there.'

'I don't think so,' said Martin. He unbuttoned Clyde's shirt, the wearer almost comatose on his feet. There was a passport size pouch against his chest. 'I saw the cord round his neck. Let's see what's in there.'

He took the pouch off Clyde's neck, unzipped it and looked inside. Martin took out the objects one at a time.

'Passport, credit card and, oh yes, here we are, an airline ticket. Valid for one month to Vancouver.'

'I'll try to get him on a flight, must be one soon, do you think?'

'Mid week, single passenger, Heathrow... You'll get him on all right. Just hope there's a flight. But they won't take him drunk.'

'It's a few hours to Heathrow. I hope he'll be sober enough.'

Martin put the items back in the pouch which he put back around Clyde's neck. He did the shirt buttons up.

'I'll need petrol for the journey,' said Jack.

'Take fifty,' said Martin, taking notes from the wallet. 'There's no tens. OK, take sixty. Never mind. Here, have it.'

Jack hesitated for a second. George was dead. And George was a hit man. Little doubt there. George owed Clyde. Natural justice. Jack took the money.

'Thanks.'

'It's not mine. Thank the man at Upton Park, smeared fifty yards along the train line.'

Martin assisted Jack getting Clyde to his van. He was obedient, lumberingly heavy. They jockeyed him into the passenger seat where Jack put the safety belt on him.

'Hope your mum's recovering,' he said to Martin.

'Cross fingers. Safe journey, Clyde.'

He patted him on the shoulder. Clyde grinned sheepishly, eyes closed. Impossible to know what he was hearing.

'See you, Jack.'

Martin gave a wave and left, heading for the hospital entrance.

Jack went round to the driver's side of his van. Once inside, he put on his seat belt. Clyde had dozed off, a sweetish boozy smell coming off him. Let him sleep it away. It would take him maybe two hours to get to Heathrow, depending on traffic. Clyde needed the time. They wouldn't let him on a flight in this state.

Jack sat back, thinking what he'd done. It had been a tempestuous hour. He hadn't killed anyone. Not directly. In fact, saved Clyde's life from an assailant who was about to push him in front of a train. Leaving George pushing at plain air. Which doesn't push back.

Was he to blame for George's death? All he'd done was pull Clyde to safety. And there'd been the unintended consequence of George falling on the line. He hadn't seen him. His concern had been Clyde, standing precariously at the edge of the platform. Who maybe was going to jump and maybe not. Jack thought not, being so far drunk, likely Clyde's decision making would have been too slow.

He couldn't evade some guilt himself. He'd played a part in a violent death. Then again, if he hadn't been there, Clyde would be dead, pushed by George into the path of the incoming train.

In another world, in another universe.

He had assisted in the death of a hit man. Not caused it, as he hadn't pushed George. Just taken away the barrier. How many lives had he saved in future years? If George had a hit every three months, every six months... Unknowable. He was dead.

A death Jack had falsified. That had to be a crime. He had shoved Clyde's wallet onto the line, so the investigators would think the body was Clyde. Had anyone spotted him? There were lots of people about. CCTV was unlikely to have caught his sneaky shove. Half the time they weren't working or too far off.

And to keep his crimes going, he was stealing 60 quid from George. The dead rat. It wasn't George's any more. It was his inheritors'. But not Jack's. He could justify it easily enough. George was out to kill Clyde, so owed him something. But the law was a stickler, if this should ever come to court.

Who would tell on him? Clyde didn't know what was going on. But Martin did.

Not good putting himself in Martin's hands. Then again, Martin had George's credit card. So Jack had as much on him as he had on Jack. But if Martin was arrested for using George's card, then Jack had nothing on him.

Rest on the fact, things had to be proved. He had been given cash from George's wallet by Martin. That was deniable. They could call each other liars and nothing could be done. But if it should come about that the investigators had doubts about who the body on the line was... Well, Clyde's fingerprints were on the wallet Jack had pushed on the tracks.

But so were his own.

Not altogether comfortable, Jack set off for Heathrow.

Chapter 33

Off the North Circular Road at Brent Cross, Jack pulled in for petrol. Clyde was asleep, snoring loudly enough to raise the roof. Jack had tried drowning it out with the radio, but the snoring won out.

The van's tank filled, he went for a coffee, buying two, in case Clyde should wake, and the old standby, a tube of peppermints. He drank his coffee in the van, the other on the dashboard, before setting off again. Clyde's head was slumped almost onto his chest as he snored. Jack checked the time on the phone, just after four o'clock. He'd be hitting the rush hour soon. Nothing he could do about that but hoped the traffic didn't jam up. Not that he had any timetable. He didn't know the times of flights, he had nothing to rush back for.

Not a meal to cook for Beryl, which had been a worry with his lack of culinary skills. Such a long day. He hoped Cleo was OK.

And here he was getting Clyde out of the country. Unlikely he was a suspect in Beryl's death. George could have been, but what would have been the motive?

Jack finished his coffee and started off. The sudden movement woke Clyde.

'Where are we?' he said.

'On the North Circular Road, on the way to Heathrow.'

'I haven't got my suitcase,' said Clyde.

'You have. It's in the van.'

He turned back into the stream of traffic. The route was easy enough. He would continue this way until he hit the

M4, then take the M4 to the airport. Satnav was for sissies. Though he had to say that, not having one.

'I was at Upton Park station,' said Clyde, flicking his eyes to get used to the light. 'I was going to go somewhere. Can't remember where.'

'There's a coffee on the dashboard for you.'

'Thank you.' He took it, removed the lid and sipped. 'Nice and sugary. Just the way I like it. Not good for diabetics... Something happened at Upton Park.'

'Clyde Rogers died.'

'I'm here. I don't understand you.'

'Where's your wallet?'

Clyde searched his pockets.

'I haven't got it. It's gone.'

'It's on the line at Upton Park,' said Jack, 'along with a black man mashed to pieces when he fell in front of a train.'

'Who fell?'

'You were on the edge of the platform, too close, so I pulled you out the way as the train was coming in. But George went to push you, missed and fell on to the track.'

'He's dead?'

'One hundred per cent.'

'Let me get this straight. I'm a bit fuzzy. You are telling me George is dead?'

'Run over by a train.'

'OK, if a train hit him, he's dead. I get that. But you said Clyde Rogers is dead.' He patted his chest. 'This isn't heaven or hell, I'm still around.'

'Martin's a pickpocket. He'd taken George's ID. So I put yours on the line in its place.'

Clyde drank his coffee, his brow wrinkled in bemusement.

'There can't be two Clyde Rogers,' he said. 'One on the track at Upton Park, one getting on a plane at Heathrow.'

'Who's going to connect them?'

Clyde thought about it.

'Maybe they won't. Just another suicide on the tracks,' he said. 'I was thinking of doing it, you know.'

'I could see that.'

The road ahead was busier, traffic coming in from every side road. The rush hour was on. Ahead of them was a supermarket lorry, and the traffic too packed for Jack to overtake.

'George was following me,' mused Clyde. 'No one would believe me. The Fergusons were employing him, I am sure of it. They want me dead for being a witness.'

'They'll think you're dead now.'

'I hope you're right. But what will they think has happened to George?'

'Guys like George make enemies. Maybe he had to head to Spain in a hurry. Disappear for whatever reason. But Clyde's dead, and that's what the Fergusons wanted. George is another matter. We can't say who will be looking for him. Or when.'

They drove on, not speaking for a while. Clyde had plenty to dwell on. His death especially, and whether that freed him or not.

He broke the silence.

'My family, back here. They'll think I'm dead.'

There was nothing Jack could say to that. They would indeed. It was not just the Fergusons who'd be fooled.

'Maybe that's OK,' said Clyde quietly. 'I've been dead for them, more or less. I can only live one life. I was going to kill myself and end it. It's just my sister, she'll be cut up at my death. My mother doesn't know anything. Hardly here at all. In a few days, she'll be buried. It's only my sister I care about.'

'She'd prefer you to be alive.'

'I can't tell her. I got to be dead. Dead to the Fergusons. Sorry, sis. Has to be done, it's the only way I can go. I died under a train at Upton Park. Thanks, Jack. I've a long flight to Vancouver ahead. I shall stay sober. I promise you. These were my drunken days. Done and gone. London was one big bottle. But the drunk fell under a train. In Canada, maybe I can save my marriage. One place, one town. This one has burnt down. I won't be the ghost at the feast, I'll live my life. You have given me a chance. More than I deserve. I'll take it. This one I won't blow.'

'I believe you,' said Jack.

It was possible. Always possible. But so was the reverse. He'd heard too many brave speeches at Alcohol Halt from declaimers whose resolve hadn't lasted a week. But there were a few, a very few, who had stuck with it.

It was always possible.

Chapter 34

Fayyad and Hayley were seated at Cleo's bedside. Much of the electronic equipment had been removed. Fayyad had told Martin to wait outside while they questioned his mother.

'How are you, Cleo?' said Fayyad.

The back of the bed had been lifted, supporting her on the pillows. She was pale, her curly hair tied back in a band, and wearing a pale blue hospital robe. On the bedside cabinet was a large bunch of yellow and red chrysanthemums in a vase.

'Not too bad, all considered,' she said. 'A little weak. They tell me I can go home tomorrow.'

'That's good,' said Fayyad. 'You're recovering quickly.'

She leaned forward and took a glass of water from the array on the shelf by her bed.

'I've been told to drink lots of water,' she said, taking a long draught. 'I was poisoned, you know.'

'We do know,' said Fayyad. 'With this.' He held up his phone to show a photo of a brown bottle. 'Do you recognise it?'

'Yes. It's the bottle I found in George's room.'

'Why did you take it?'

'I didn't trust him. I found him searching Clyde's room. Yesterday, before Beryl...' She flapped a hand as if to dismiss that business. 'He told me he was a private detective investigating Clyde, who was a big criminal. And you lot were useless.'

'We've been called worse,' said Fayyad. 'But the bottle...' he reminded her.

'I thought his story was fishy. So I had a look in George's room when he was out. I found the bottle, taped under the wardrobe, would you believe. I thought this must be important. So I took it.'

'How did you come to ingest it?'

'Not deliberately. Nothing like that. It was later, I'd been busy vacuuming and whatnot. I went back to my room and found it lying on its side. Got knocked over somehow. And leaking. I wiped it off and tightened the top. Must've got some on my fingers. Licked them. I should have been wearing gloves. Can it really be so poisonous?'

'So we are told.'

'I remember an odd taste. Yesterday, mid morning. Like vinegary pineapple.' She shuddered. 'But I was fine all day. I did the barbecue last night, no problem, breakfast this morning. Found Beryl, her head bashed in, heaven help me. You lot came. I remember all that. And then nothing until I woke up here about two hours ago.'

'You were given the antidote,' said Fayyad. 'It was found in George's room. We brought it to the hospital.'

'Blessings for that. I am so grateful. Definitely worked.' She took another sip of water. 'Nasty stuff.' And shuddered again. 'What did George want with it?'

'That's what we'd like to know,' said Fayyad. 'We'll pick him up, and find out what he has to say.'

'Such a palaver,' said Cleo. 'And I'm stuck here. There must be customers phoning. I'm losing business. My phone's back at the house, I hope. I don't know where I am without it. One hand stirring the soup, the other holding the phone to my ear. How much longer are you going to be there?'

'The crime scene manager expects to leave tomorrow afternoon.'

'I'll have to throw out the carpet in Beryl's room...' She was biting her thumb at the thought of all the tasks to be done, the business lost.

'They've taken the blood stained area away as evidence,' said Hayley.

'I can't afford to be ill,' she exclaimed. 'And that room! Who's going to want to sleep in it? Have to be me. Can't inflict it on a guest.'

'Tell us about your relationship with Beryl,' said Fayyad.

'Horrible woman. I've got to say it. They say speak no ill of the dead, but she was abominable. Blackmailing me. Making pots of money in her job but squeezing me dry. I'm glad she's dead. There, I've said it. And I don't care who hears it.'

'What was she blackmailing you for?'

'Tax. I have to admit it. You're going through my accounts, aren't you?'

'We are.'

'Oh, what a mess! I don't know how I am going to get out of it.'

'Get yourself a tax advisor,' said Hayley.

'What with?' exclaimed Cleo. 'I haven't got a brass farthing. I'm overdrawn to my limit.'

'How did it start with Beryl?' said Fayyad. 'The black-mail.'

'She offered to do my annual audit cheap. I should never have accepted it. But stupidly, I did. And I wasn't as clever as I thought I'd been... She found out I had been underpaying tax for too long. Ages. Years.'

'You've not been paying her money, though.'

'No money. But she was staying free. The cow. And her brother half rate. And then she wanted him free too. How was I to make a living with that pair of leeches taking all the profit?'

'It's a strong motive to kill her.'

'I didn't. I found her body, sure. But didn't kill her. I was preparing breakfast with Martin. Feeding the house, how would I have time to kill her? Much as I would have liked to.'

'You could have conspired with Martin.'

'You saying he did it for me?'

'Yes.'

'He was working with me in the kitchen, for heaven's sake. Cooking, serving. We were busy with breakfast. You think I said to him: Martin dear, when you've finished laying the table, go up to room 2 and smash Beryl on the head. There's a good boy. Then wash your hands, come down and make the toast.' She threw up her hands. 'Enough. Please leave me be. I was at death's door. I am recovering. I've nothing more to tell you.'

Chapter 35

It was past eight o'clock and getting dark when Jack arrived home from Heathrow. Hungry, he made himself beans on toast. That would do. He had been tempted to get a takeaway as he had money left even after the extortionate Heathrow parking charge. But had resisted.

Wholemeal bread, at least, nothing fried. Beans were OK, weren't they?

But the journey back, the traffic! Who'd be a taxi driver?

Jack had stayed with Clyde at the terminal for over an hour, making sure he was OK. Clyde managed to get a seat on a flight which should be in the air by now.

Clyde had been upbeat, saying how he was going to change his life, be a new person. Jack hadn't argued, what was the point? But he'd heard such high blown statements too many times. Admittedly, Clyde had the strongest of motives, being alive when he could've been dead.

But alcoholics mostly overestimate their strength. He'd love to be wrong. And there would be an upbeat Vancouver story. Jack had done all he could this side of the pond.

Finishing his meal, still a little hungry, maybe something later, Jack decided to shower, then perhaps phone the hospital about Cleo, and watch some TV. It had been a long day. Next to no work done, but it certainly felt like he'd been breaking rocks the live long day.

His phone rang. Mia. Someone he'd forgotten, what with the happenings at Upton Park station and getting Clyde on a plane.

'Hello, Mia. How's it going?'

'I tried to phone you earlier but your phone was off.'

'I drove a friend to the airport.' He'd almost said Clyde, but Clyde was dead. 'I turn my phone off in the van. What have you got to tell me?'

There was a pause, alarming Jack.

'I gave Martin my phone number,' she said.

He, of course, knew this.

'Stupid of you,' he said.

'I am stupid,' she said. After a pause she added, 'He phoned me two hours ago.'

'What did he say?'

'He said he'd just got some money, and would I like to come out to dinner tonight?'

So much for Martin's promises.

'What did you say?'

'I said yes.' She paused to let that sink in. 'I was getting ready to go out, clothes and make up, when Mum caught me. I was in the middle of texting him. She saw it and got everything out of me. She made me phone you. This call. She's listening now.'

'He's 22 years old,' said Jack. 'You're 14. Underage sex is a criminal offence.'

'Mum's said that.'

'I'm saying it too. You're too young. Find a boy your own age.'

'They're such drips.'

'I wouldn't say you were being exactly sensible.'

'I bought condoms.'

'Oh for heaven's sake! Preparing for it.'

'Would you rather I didn't?'

'I don't want you getting pregnant, sure. But neither do I want you having sex with men a lot older than you are. In fact, you shouldn't be having sex at all. Not at your age.'

'That's exactly what Mum said.'

'I shall tell Martin what's what when I see him.'

'You needn't bother, Mum's spoken to him. Or should I say shouted at him. Blasted his ears off.'

Jack couldn't help a smile. He knew Alison at full fury.

'She told him that she had his name,' she continued in a bored dirge, 'and his phone number, she'd call the police etc etc. She told him I was well underage, that he couldn't say he didn't know. She said he was a beast, a pervert, an animal...'

'I'd better talk to your mum.'

Jack didn't want to speak to his ex but it was unavoidable. He could hear her voice off, but couldn't make out the words.

Mia came back on. 'She says she'll talk to you tomorrow when she's calmed down.'

That was a relief. Alison would blame him for taking Mia to the barbecue and not keeping an eye on her. Which was true, as at the time he'd been keeping an eye on Beryl.

'So I'm not going out with him tonight,' went on Mia. 'Or any night. And I've said more than enough. You know, Mum knows. And Martin has been ordered never to phone me again. And please, please, don't say anything. Or I shall evaporate from the face of the earth.'

'Sounds like you've got the message.'

'Loud and clear. Goodnight, Dad.'

The call ended.

Jack was seated on the arm of his sofa. Quite a phone call. He wondered how Alison had got her to phone him. Threatened to take her phone away for life if she didn't. Something like that. Mia would give up an arm to keep her phone.

And as for Martin. That lying dog. Of course he'd picked tonight to ask her out. He had money courtesy of George. His mother was in hospital, so he could use George's room as that was vacant. The bastard. He had promised on his mother's life to stay away from Mia.

What a louse! A pickpocket, and heaven knows what else.

Jack was still swearing at him as he showered.

Martin had slept with Beryl last night. He was young and good looking; he had no trouble attracting women his own age or older, so why go for Mia?

Sex is sex. And why is rarely a useful question. You can ask it till the cows come home. It won't get you anywhere.

He was drying himself and thinking of last night. Martin sleeping with Beryl, Larry in the tent as his wife, Jean, had commandeered his room. Jack saw his own grubby t-shirt on the floor of his bathroom, the one that he'd been wearing all day. And it hit him.

The t-shirt and the tent.

Dried and dressed, he phoned Fayyad.

Chapter 36

Jack walked down his road to the B&B. At the door was a policeman in uniform. A youngish man, obviously bored. He perked up when he saw Jack.

'No one's allowed in the house, sir, except guests and the owner. I have a list.' He indicated his notebook. 'Might you be on it?'

'I'm not,' said Jack. 'I'm here to meet Detective Sergeant Fayyad Kamani.'

'Sorry, sir, but I haven't been notified. If he's due, you'll have to wait out here for him.'

The policeman's phone rang. He put it to his ear.

'Yes sir,' he said into the phone. 'I think he's here right now.' He said to Jack, 'Can I have your name, sir?'

'Jack Bell.'

The policeman gave a thumbs up to Jack as he spoke into the phone. 'He's here, sir. I'll tell him.' He closed the call. 'DS Kamani will be a little late, sir. He's searching for a metal detector. I'm to let you in the lounge but nowhere else.'

'The lounge will be fine. Thank you.'

Jack followed him into the house, down the hallway and into the lounge at the rear of the house. Martin and Larry were there. Of course, he enumerated, just the two of them. Cleo was in hospital, Jean had given up on Larry and left, Clyde was flying to Vancouver, Beryl was in the mortuary, and what was left of George was probably there too.

The policeman left them.

'Hello, Jack,' said Martin.

He was in jeans, t-shirt and denim jacket, the same clothes he'd been wearing earlier, the good looking boy-o. He needed a shave which probably added to his appeal.

Jack marched up to him and grabbed him by the lapels.

'Stay away from my daughter. Do you hear!'

Martin pushed him away angrily.

'I haven't been anywhere near your precious daughter.'

'You phoned her. You asked her out for dinner. Don't deny it. She told me.'

'I thought better of it. I cancelled. And you've no cause to have a go at me. All the money I gave you.'

It struck Jack, the position he'd put himself in. Taking a dead man's money from Martin, when only he and Martin, and of course Clyde, knew the man under the train was George. Not one to be obligated to, when the young man knew who had planted Clyde's ID on the corpse.

'Stay away from Mia,' he said. 'You made me a promise.'

'I'll be keeping it. Just don't heavy me.' He eyed Jack from two metres away. 'I got enough on you. Don't play the big man.'

'Stay away from her.'

'Or you'll do what? Tell my mum?'

Jack took a deep breath. He had no threats worth anything.

'You're a good looking guy, Martin,' he said, trying to be reasonable. 'I'm sure you have no trouble attracting women your own age. Why go for jail bait?'

Martin shrugged. 'Sure I can get women. But it's what you fancy that matters.' He turned to Larry who was seated in an armchair reading. 'Isn't that so, Larry?'

'Don't involve me.'

'Oh come on.' Martin strolled up to him and slapped him on the shoulder. 'Just before Jack came you were telling me you liked 'em young.'

'That's a lie, Jack.' He put the book down on the arm of the chair. 'A filthy lie.'

Martin smirked. 'Come on, Larry. You were giving me details, places you'd been to pick up schoolgirls...'

'He's lying, Jack. I was reading a book.'

He held up the book as if it could be used in court.

'Just shut up, Martin,' Jack said sharply. 'I thought you an OK guy this afternoon. Don't add poison.'

'It's my way,' said Martin with a shrug. 'I get bored. So bored, I even slept with his sister.'

'How dare you!' exclaimed Larry. 'Dead less than a day and you speak like that of her.'

'It's my manner, man. Say it like it is.' He smiled brightly at Jack. 'Don't take any notice of me, Jack. I get stupid. I say dumb things. None of it true. Not for long, anyway.'

You make enemies, thought Jack. You leave town in a hurry.

'If the cops weren't here,' went on Martin, 'I'd go and score some weed. But with them around, I'll settle for TV.'

He swaggered out of the room, daring them to challenge him.

'He's a liar,' hissed Larry. 'I was reading.' He held up the book as evidence, *Three Men in a Boat*.

'It's OK, I believe you,' he said, not knowing whether to or not. It was immaterial. 'Let's kill the subject.'

'I just came in here for a quiet read,' said Larry.

He was wearing the clothes he'd been working in that morning: t-shirt, dress trousers and smart shoes. A strange combination.

'They won't let you in your room?' said Jack.

'No,' said Larry. 'I need to shower and change. There's crime scene people still upstairs. All this time. Won't even let me out in the garden for a smoke.'

'They have to do their job,' said Jack.

'I understand that,' said Larry. 'But I feel so scruffy.'

The front door opened and then slammed. Jack went to the lounge door and opened it. In the hallway was Fayyad with a metal detector over his shoulder.

'The trouble I had digging this out,' he said as he came into the lounge.

'Can I go up to my room?' said Larry. 'I need to change and wash.'

Fayyad called back down the hallway:

'George! Escort Mr Taylor upstairs. See if the CSIs have done with his room.'

The police constable beckoned Larry, who left the room. Fayyad closed the door. He put down the metal detector, and sat on the arm of an armchair.

Jack was on the sofa facing him.

'Before I hear from you, I've some news for you,' said Fayyad. 'About Clyde.'

'What's that?'

'He fell under a train at Upton Park. It's quite likely he jumped.'

'Poor man.'

'Yes, indeed. Poor man. His body was ground under the wheels like mince meat. He could only be ID'd from his wallet photo card. I'm sure it was suicide. When we interviewed him this morning, he was like a dead man walking. I thought, he's not going to live long, not in that state. So there you are. Sad news.' He sighed. 'I'm too often the messenger, Jack. But he's nothing to do with Beryl's murder, unless you know of a connection?'

'None,' said Jack. 'But I know who did the murder.'

'Then you'd best put me in the picture.'

'It's the tent. Martin's tent, out there. I came in this morning about 7.40. Larry was already working, he was wearing the clothes he had on at the barbecue: a pink shirt, dress trousers, and shiny leather shoes. He couldn't change as he'd slept in the tent and his wife was occupying his room. The light woke him up, he said, so he'd started work early. He'd been bringing in sand from the drive and raking it. Doing it, I would think, for at least half an hour before I arrived. He showed me one of the forms was out.'

'What's a form?'

'Wood sides to make a mould for concrete. I had put in four forms to hold the concrete for the shed base. They have to be exactly level. And one wasn't, with a couple of pegs displaced. We reckoned it had been done the night before, someone at the barbecue had accidentally kicked it over. But it had to be put back properly as we were aiming to lay the concrete today. So I went out to the van, took a wheelbarrow as I might as well bring back a load of sand. At the van, I got out a plank to work off, and my spirit level, but I couldn't find my hammers. My van is a bit of a mess but...'

'I've seen it. A wonder you can find anything.'

'I must've spent seven or eight minutes looking for hammers. And gave up and got a mallet instead. I filled the wheelbarrow with sand, put the plank, mallet and spirit level on top and wheeled it all back to the site. And there was Larry raking away. But he'd changed his shirt. Instead of his pink shirt, he was wearing the t-shirt he wore when he was working with me yesterday. He told me he got it from the tent; he didn't want to ruin the shirt. Anyway, we got the displaced form level again and banged in the pegs. We then wheelbarrowed in loads of sand, me and Larry, and raked them level until we were called in to breakfast.'

'So what am I here for? Sounds like you were both working when Beryl was killed.'

'That's been my thinking. Today's been busy, I've been occupied with other matters. A problem with my daughter, Cleo in hospital... Stuff.' He had no intention of mentioning Clyde and George. 'It was when I finally got home, went in the bathroom to have a shower, and there was my t-shirt on the floor. And it occurred to me, Larry's t-shirt. Why would it have been in Martin's tent?'

'And what's your answer?'

'Let's have a look at the tent.'

Chapter 37

The French windows were open, the curtains wide to maximise spillage, the patio lamp on. Fayyad and Jack were by the tent on the lawn. Jack had collected a spade from Cleo's shed at the back of her vegetable patch. Fayyad had the metal detector and a plastic box that he'd brought in from his car.

Fayyad opened the tent flaps and shone his torch round the inside. Much of the space was taken up by a sleeping bag. It lay neatly on the ground sheet, having been tidied since its last sleeper had arisen. There was a pillow at its head. Along one side of the tent were assorted items of male clothing.

'What am I looking for?' said Fayyad. 'Sweaty socks?'

'I don't think it will be inside the tent,' said Jack. 'Try a corner. That far one, I reckon.'

'What are you doing in my tent!' Martin shouted, coming rapidly over.

'Looking for my hammers,' said Jack.

'I haven't got them. Why would I want them anyway?'

'You took them for a weapon.'

'Listen to the man!' Martin was flapping his arms about to show his low opinion. 'On and on, he goes. No evidence whatsoever!'

Fayyad closed the flaps.

'Where did you say?' said Fayyad.

'Try that corner,' said Jack.

Martin was shaking his head in disbelief like a footballer admonished by the ref. He had never fouled. Never would.

Long shadows climbed the tent walls, disappearing in the purple night. Fayyad walked round the canvas to where Jack had indicated, and knelt down, feeling around the tent corner.

'There's something here, under the ground sheet. Bring the box over.'

Jack brought over the plastic box and placed it by Fayyad. He took off the lid, and carefully put on a pair of latex gloves.

'So what is it?' he said.

'I know nothing about it, whatever it is,' said Martin. 'It's been planted.'

Fayyad put a hand under the groundsheet. And pulled out a claw hammer, which he held up by the handle.

'No sign of blood on it. Is it yours, Jack?'

'I think so.'

'I know nothing about it,' said Martin.

'You took this hammer from my van yesterday,' said Jack. 'I was clearing up, going back and forth, and you took it. For a weapon.'

'Lies! Blatant lies,' declared Martin. 'He'll say anything to put me in the frame.'

'Then it won't have your prints on,' said Fayyad as he put the hammer into an evidence bag he'd taken from the box.

'There's a second hammer,' said Jack. 'Still missing.'

'The murder weapon?' said Fayyad.

'I think so.'

'I know nothing about it,' exclaimed Martin. 'I did not take his hammers.'

'I heard you the first time,' said Fayyad.

'You took the hammers out of my van when I was out of sight,' said Jack. 'Two hammers. Let's find the second.'

'He's making this up!' yelled Martin. 'I don't know anything about hammers. Or where they are.'

'Let's look at the site,' said Jack.

They crossed the lawn to Jack's workings. Fayyad had the torch and metal detector, Jack the spade and the box with its various items including the claw hammer in the evidence bag. Martin followed from a distance, still complaining.

The site was sand covered, smoothly raked to the forms, lit obliquely by the lights from the lounge and patio, throwing across it the long thin shadows of the approaching walkers.

Fayyad handed the torch to Jack. He took up the metal detector.

'Let's see if I can remember what I was told, on how to use this,' he said. 'So what are we looking for?'

'My club hammer,' said Jack.

The metal detector consisted of a pole with a circular flat end, about the size of a dinner plate which would scour the ground. At the top of the pole was a handle. Attached to the handle was a small screen which indicated the depth and type of metal found.

'The fanciest one I've seen,' said Jack. 'You should be in a space suit on the moon.'

'It wasn't cheap,' said Fayyad. 'We don't buy any old rubbish, you know. Whatever we find might be needed for evidential purposes.'

'As this may be.'

Martin was standing back, interested, but pretending not to be. Larry had come out of the French windows onto the patio. He was watching Jack and Fayyad, the latter with the metal detector. Larry was hesitant, trying to work out what they were doing, what they might find in the workings.

He crossed the lawn to them.

Fayyad had strapped the machine to his forearm and was holding the handle. He switched the detector on. It hummed like a small insect.

'All set to find hidden treasure,' he said, and stepped onto the levelled sand.

'You'll mess it up!' yelled Larry. 'All my raking.'

'We can rake it again,' said Jack. 'No hassle.'

'What are you looking for?'

'What do you think?' said Jack.

'You don't need to mess up the sand. My raking. I hate a mess. Please, leave it be.'

He stepped onto the sand and grasped the handle of the metal detector.

'Let go,' said Fayyad. 'Whatever is here, it will find it.'

Larry reluctantly let go. He looked around bewildered, like a frightened animal. He had washed and wore a clean white shirt. Fayyad was criss-crossing the sand with the metal detector. Larry stood in front of him.

'Look at this mess. Stop. I'll show you.' He took a few steps and took the spade from Jack. 'There's no need for this mess. I had it perfect. Please get off.'

Fayyad hesitated for an instant, then stepped off the sand with the metal detector.

Larry went round the site to one corner of the workings and began digging with the spade, taking out the sand carefully so as not to excessively enlarge the hole. All the time standing on the grass, just beyond the form, so as not to mess up more raked sand than was necessary.

'We had it perfect,' he said.

'Spoiling my fun,' said Fayyad, watching Larry dig. 'I was looking forward to the click of the machine.'

He laid it on the grass.

Larry put down the spade and dropped to his knees, a few inches from the form. He began scrabbling at the sand with his hands. The edge of a bag appeared, he scooped the sand from round it, carefully as if it were an archaeological artefact. Then pulled it free, sand falling away as he lifted it up like treasure trove.

It was a transparent plastic bag containing a club hammer and a crumpled pink cloth.

'I'll have that,' said Fayyad. He had put on a fresh pair of latex gloves while Larry had been digging. Taking the bag from Larry, he held it up for all to see. 'There are two witnesses who have seen that you knew exactly where to find it.'

'Three,' said Martin, a little way back.

'Three witnesses,' Fayyad corrected himself. 'There's a club hammer inside. And with it a shirt.' He turned the bag round. 'A bloodstained shirt.'

'Larry was wearing that shirt this morning,' said Jack, 'when I arrived. About 15 minutes later, he had changed into a t-shirt. He told me he got the t-shirt from the tent.' Jack turned to Larry. 'Why should your t-shirt have been in Martin's tent, Larry?'

'Why do you think?' said Larry, still on his knees, as if looking into the hole for salvation. 'You seem to know. Tell them.'

'The t-shirt wasn't in the tent. How could it be? You lied to me, to all of us, Larry, saying that it was.'

'Why would I do that?'

'Because you didn't want to admit that you'd been in the house. You wanted to make it seem as if you'd had a quick change of shirt from the tent. That was all. Then gone back to raking. But instead, you'd gone into the house and murdered your sister.'

Jack stopped his narration to watch Larry's reaction. Martin had come in closer, realising he was off the hook. Fayyad was scratching his chin, a thinking cop's pose.

'How did Larry have time?' he said.

'I was searching for my hammers, maybe seven, even eight, nine minutes. I had all my stuff on the pavement while I searched. I had to put it back. Then I was loading up sand. I could have been away eleven or twelve minutes.

Time enough for Larry to go in the house with the club hammer and smash his sister's head in.'

'With one of the hammers,' said Fayyad. 'From the tent.'

'Martin had taken them from my van. My claw hammer and my club hammer...'

'Total tosh,' exclaimed Martin. 'Keep me out of this.'

Jack ignored him. 'Martin had them for a weapon. Beryl was to be the victim. But it didn't play out. Last night, he slept with Beryl. But the hammers were in the tent where he'd left them, where Larry slept. So another night, another day for Martin. No rush. Larry, though, is in the tent. In quite a state with all that's going on. His wife's here, everyone knows he's jobless and been pretending the last couple of months. It's maybe five thirty this morning, the sun is coming up. He's found the hammers, and he knows they are mine. And lying there, in the tent as it is getting light, he comes up with a plan to get me searching for my hammers. He would move a form and pegs on the site, blame it on barbecue guests, knowing I must get the forms level for the concrete to go in. And I would want a hammer for that. Which I wouldn't find. And the search would delay me long enough for him...'

'It did,' declared Larry. 'It most surely did.'

'My claw hammer you hid under the groundsheet,' said Jack. 'You didn't need it. The club hammer was your choice. And then when I came, and began my futile search in the van for hammers, you went into the house and killed Beryl.'

'Splashing blood on his shirt,' interjected Fayyad, 'so he goes to his room, to change into the dirty t-shirt.' Fayyad flicked his fingers. 'But wasn't his wife in his room...'

'She was having a shower,' said Larry grudgingly. 'I could hear the water running from the room. I had the key, it was my room. Just a few seconds...'

'You didn't have long,' said Jack. 'You couldn't be sure how soon I'd give up searching. So, you come running out of the house, and you don't have many options. You are carrying a blood stained shirt and the club hammer. There was no way you could have left either of them in your room as the police would find them. The tent's no good. Quite a panic, I am sure. I am due back with the wheelbarrow and tools imminently...'

'So you bury the hammer and shirt in the sand,' exclaimed Fayyad. He held up the evidence bag. 'I am sure the shirt has Beryl's blood on it as well as your DNA from skin cells. I am now going to caution you.'

The police constable had come out of the French windows as if on call, and joined them at the site. Larry was seated on the grass, near the hole he'd dug in the sand as if wanting to tidy it up again. The others grouped around him in a semi-circle.

'I am arresting you, Larry Taylor,' said Fayyad, 'for the murder of Beryl Taylor. You do not have to say anything. But it may harm your defence if you do not mention when questioned something which you later rely on in court. Anything you do say may be given in evidence.'

'I killed her,' he said calmly, looking up for the first time, a half smile on his face. 'You have the evidence. I am not going to fight it and be tabloid fodder. You have everything in that plastic bag to prove your case.' He looked at them all, ensuring he had their attention. 'I had it so well planned, Jack. The burial in the sand was temporary. I was going to throw the club hammer in the river, bury the shirt ten miles from here, but I couldn't get out to the garden. The police came too quickly.'

'Not so quickly,' said Jack. 'Cleo and I didn't let on at breakfast that Beryl was dead. She didn't want anyone leaving as she knew it had to be someone round the table.'

'I knew what you'd seen,' said Larry, 'but I couldn't leap up and go out into the garden and get rid of the evidence. Not with everyone watching. Perhaps I should have done.

Slipped the claw hammer back in Jack's van, and run off with the club hammer and t-shirt. But the longer I thought of it, the less time I had to do it. And then the law arrived. And it was too late.' He closed his eyes and shook his head. 'How I wanted to get out into the garden, but you locked the French windows, had cops and guys in plastic suits everywhere.'

'To prevent evidence being removed,' said Fayyad.

Larry looked to Jack. 'I had you fooled. I thought, if I can't get out into the garden to dispose of the club hammer and shirt, then at least we can bury them in cement. Except you worked it out. I wouldn't have expected that as a builder.' He laughed, absently filling the hole he'd taken the items out of. 'I so liked working with you, Jack. Manual work. Doing something useful. Raking is therapeutic. Buddhist monks do it. With beds of stones. Back and forth like the waves on the sea.'

He was picking up sand and letting it run through his fingers, half in shadow, half lit up in the angled light from the patio.

'Why did you do it?' said Jack.

Larry looked at him, and smirked.

'Because Beryl was my sister. Because I was tired of being her brother. I am ten years older than her. I had to babysit her when I was a teenager. How I hated that. Our parents were working so I had to take her to school and pick her up. She was always there, holding me back, stopping me going out with the other lads. When I got into butterfly collecting, she had to do it too. And she was better than me at it. Better at identifying them. So I gave it up. And what do you know, a few months later, so did she.' He laughed. 'She only wanted to do it to be better than me at it.'

He put his hands behind his head and looked up at the sky. Out into a universe where none of this was happening.

'I married Jean, you know,' he said, 'because Beryl hated her. I loved watching them fight. Put the two of them in the same room and no need to light the touchpaper.' He chuckled. 'Better than cock fighting.'

'Beryl had it all. Looks, brains,' he went on. 'Cute as a water lily. She shot past me as if I was motionless. The best of marks in everything. A prime job, promotion on promotion. She was about to become a partner, you know. Slept with half of them, maybe all of them. But she looked after me. She got me half rate here, my little sister, and was going to get me zero rate. So much gratitude she was due.'

He shook his head. And shrugged.

'I was fired for what they found on my computer. Porn and call girl sites. Stupid. You don't have to tell me. No way would I ever get another job, not with the reference they'd give me. But Beryl comes to my aid. My little sister. She says don't worry, Larry, I'll employ you freelance. Can you imagine that? Me working for her. Big brother under orders. Well, I had another option. She had a house, savings, quite a few smart investments. With her dead, I'd inherit the lot. Never have to work. And I'd shut her up. No more gratitude. Think of that. Never having to say thank you to my little sister.'

Chapter 38

The cement mixer was chugging. Jack looked in at the lumpy porridge being thrown back and forth. Done. He turned off the machine, took up his shovel and shovelled a load onto the concrete already laid down. And again, and again. The level was almost up to the top of the forms. This would be the last load.

Cleo came out of the French windows. She was wearing a long black coat, unbuttoned, a black dress visible under it, black high heels and black kid gloves. Her hair was in a purple scarf and she was discreetly made up.

She crossed the lawn to him. He watched her approach and could imagine her in her dancing days, she still had that elegance once out of her apron.

'There were only ten of us there,' she said. 'I thought I ought to go.'

'I couldn't leave the concreting,' he said, leaning on the shovel. 'It has to be done in one go. And I hardly knew him. Not since school, anyway.'

'Well, I didn't know Clyde either, when it comes to it. He only stayed here a couple of nights. Didn't speak much. But he was my guest and the family invited me to his funeral. I didn't know anyone there, but they thanked me for coming. They said it was the second in a week; his mother died too.'

'Things all happen at once,' he said, for something to say.

'His sister was in bits. She looked so like him. Dido is her name. I had a bit part in Marlow's *Tragedy of Dido*. I couldn't stop thinking of it. She read a poem, the sister, so painful to watch the poor woman. She could hardly get through it, the tears rolling down her cheeks. Do you know the one? *Do Not Go Gentle into that Good Night.*'

'I've heard it,' he said. Or had he?

'Well, I did my duty,' said Cleo. 'Took some flowers.'

'Cremated, was he?'

'Yes. The little doors opened, the coffin went into the lift, the doors closed.' She shuddered. 'I'd hate to have looked into the coffin. Just bits of him scraped off the railway line.'

Gone, he thought. Burnt to cinders. Thank God for that. Impossible to prove the body wasn't Clyde's. No DNA left behind, all gone up in smoke. Little danger of Martin being believed if he tried anything. Would the witness protection programme realise something was up? How much did they keep an eye on old cases? Would they even hear of a run of the mill suicide at Upton Park? Even if they did, they couldn't betray Clyde, who was in Vancouver. Sober, he hoped.

'I'll make us some tea,' she said. 'Toast with it?'

'Wholemeal,' he said.

'I will pay you, Jack, you know,' she said. 'For the work. It's just, you'll have to wait a few weeks. I'm making more money, now that Beryl and Larry are gone. I can't let her room, well, not for a while, but I'm sleeping in it. I'm not superstitious. I can't afford to be.'

'Money dictates,' he said. 'I know all about that. Heard anything from Martin?'

'He's off on his travels again. I have no idea where.' She flapped a hand to indicate the far distance. 'He comes, he goes. I don't know where he got the money from. He came back without a penny to his name.' She shrugged. 'I do love to see him but I'm sure he gets up to things I don't want to know about.'

204

Jack could have told her some of them, but said nothing. Mothers are loath to believe the worst from their sons. She'd argue, defend her son and resent Jack. So why needlessly offend her? Martin was gone, hopefully for another two years at least, what was the point in having her worry about things she couldn't affect?

'There's a film,' she said, 'that I want to see at the Stratford Picture House...' She was shuffling on her heels a little nervously. 'I wondered if you'd like to come.'

'I would,' he said. His eagerness a giveaway, as he hadn't even asked her what film.

'That's good.' She smiled. 'I thought you might have someone else.'

'I'm in the waiting room,' he said.

'Your name has just come up on the screen. There it is.' She pointed out the imaginary screen. 'Jack Bell, please go to the Picture House. And my name too. Isn't technology wonderful. Enough. I talk too much when I'm excited.' She touched him on the hand. 'I am so pleased to get my rooms back. Paying rooms, I mean.'

Her gloved hand rested a second. Jack squeezed a finger, leaving a line of cement dust on the black leather. Their eyes lingered. Jack might have kissed her but she eased away.

'I'll make the tea and toast. We'll have it in the lounge. Bit chilly out here. I'll give you a call.'

She blew him a kiss through a glove as she walked away.

He watched her go through the French windows, gazing until there was no chance of her coming back. He touched his hand where she'd touched him. Time enough. A film show, and who knows what in the days to come.

Work to be done.

Jack levelled the concrete he'd just poured in with the shovel. Thick and lumpy, like a grey pudding. He got down

205

on his knees, and with the edge of a plank that crossed the forms, he scraped the surface.

He stood back. It would dry in a week, and then he'd assemble the summerhouse.

'Tea, Jack!' she called.

Thank you!

I am grateful to every reader who finishes one of my novels. I have taken you on a journey which I hope you have enjoyed. There are plenty of things you could have been doing, other than reading this book. So, thank you for your time.

If you liked *Jack at the Lodge,* here's what you can do next:

I'd appreciate a review on Amazon. In that way, you can help me tell other readers about my books. Without reviews authors get few sales on Amazon. So I'd be grateful for your review to help this series get on the move.

You can get a FREE ebook of *Jack of Spades* or *Murder at Any Price* if you sign up for my readers' list. You may give it to a friend if you wish. When you sign up for my readers' list you will receive my regular newsletter. This will give you news about me, what I'm reading, and tell you about my future books, PLUS a variety of giveaways.

Sign up at my website:

DerekSmithWriter.com

Books by DH Smith

Jack Bell
These are all standalone novels and can be read in any order. They are:

Jack of All Trades

Jack of Spades

Jack o'Lantern

Jack By The Hedge

Jack In The Box

Jack On The Tower

Jack Recalled

Jack At Death's Door

Jack At The Gate

Jack In The Dust

Jack At The Lodge

Other Books
Murder at Any Price

Writing A Crime Novel

Books by Derek Smith

All my books, other than the Jack of All Trades series and *Murder at Any Price*, are written under the name Derek Smith.

Fantasy
Hell's Chimney
The Prince's Shadow

Other Books
Strikers of Hanbury Street (short stories)
Catching Up (poetry)

Young Adult Novels
Hard Cash
Half a Bike
Fast Food
Frances Fairweather Demon Striker!

Children's Novels
The Good Wolf
Feather Brains
Baker's Boy

For Younger Children
The Magical World of Lucy-Anne
Lucy-Anne's Changing Ways
Jack's Bus

About the Author

I live in Forest Gate in the East End of London. In my working life, I have been a plastics chemist, a gardener and a stage manager before becoming a professional writer. I began with plays, working with several theatre companies, and had a few plays on radio and TV, as well as on the stage.

In the early 80s I became involved in running a co-operative bookshop and vegetarian café in Stratford, where I learned to cook, and had my first go at writing a novel. The first was a mess, and, after too many rewrites, binned. The transition from drama to novels took me a couple of years to get to grips with.

My first success was a young adult novel, *Hard Cash*, published by Faber. Buoyed up by this, I stuck with children's work, did school visits, and made a hand to mouth living as a full time author, topped up with some evening class work in creative writing at City University and the Mary Ward Centre in Holborn. A few adult fiction titles appeared from time to time, between the children's list, and I have since been working more in that direction with my Jack of All Trades series.

DerekSmithWriter.com

The book you've been reading was designed by Lia at

Contact lia@freeyourwords.com for a quote